Loving Lizzie

Lone Wolf Generations Book 1

Alicia Montgomery

Also by Alicia Montgomery

The True Mates Series

Fated Mates

Blood Moon

Romancing the Alpha

Witch's Mate

Taming the Beast

Tempted by the Wolf

The Lone Wolf Defenders Series

Killian's Secret

Loving Quinn

All for Connor

The True Mates Standalone Novels

Holly Jolly Lycan Christmas

A Mate for Jackson: Bad Alpha Dads

True Mates Generations

A Twist of Fate

Claiming the Alpha

Alpha Ascending

A Witch in Time

Highland Wolf

Daughter of the Dragon

Shadow Wolf

A Touch of Magic

Heart of the Wolf

THE LONE WOLF GENERATIONS SERIES

Loving Lizzie

THE BLACKSTONE MOUNTAIN SERIES

The Blackstone Dragon Heir

The Blackstone Bad Dragon

The Blackstone Bear

The Blackstone Wolf

The Blackstone Lion

The Blackstone She-Wolf

The Blackstone She-Bear

The Blackstone She-Dragon

BLACKSTONE RANGERS SERIES

Blackstone Ranger Chief

Blackstone Ranger Charmer

Blackstone Ranger Hero

Blackstone Ranger Rogue

Blackstone Ranger Guardian

Blackstone Ranger Scrooge

DRAGON GUARD OF THE NORTHERN ISLES

Dragon Guard Warrior

Dragon Guard Scholar

Dragon Guard Knight

Dragon Guard Fighter

Dragon Guard Protector

Dragon Guard Crusader

Prologue

A few weeks ago ...

Using technology was as easy as breathing for Lizzie Martin.

In fact, it was practically involuntary when, at the age of seven, she had accidentally caused an ATM machine to spit out hundreds of dollars.

What exactly happened?

From what Lizzie could recall, the events of that day were as follows:

INT. NEW YORK NATIONAL BANK - DAY

LIZZIE stomps into the bank right behind MOM, and they stop by the row of ATMs near the entrance.

                                MOM
            Are you going to pout at me all day, Elizabeth Eowyn?

LIZZIE huffs and crosses her arms over her chest. MOM
sighs and looks heavenward.

                                MOM
            Lizzie, you can't have a new toy just because you want one.

                                LIZZIE
            But, Mom, it's the super special edition Tammy USA Girl
            doll! They're only making a few hundred. I have to get
                              one NOW.

                                MOM
            It's not Christmas or your birthday, you can't have one.

                                LIZZIE
                                But—

                                MOM
            No buts, young lady. (Sighs) Now, stay here, don't talk to
                    strangers, and don't touch anything!

                                LIZZIE
                                Fine.

As MOM leaves, LIZZIE leans on the ATM machine and
grumbles to herself.

                                LIZZIE

If only I had my own money, I can buy the Tammy USA Girl doll myself.

A disembodied voice answers her.

VOICE

I have money.

LIZZIE starts and looks around, but there's no one around her. The bank tellers and other customers are all the way across the room.

LIZZIE

Who said that?

There's no answer. She shrugs and leans back on the ATM.

VOICE

I said, I have the money.

LIZZIE once again jumps in surprise. She repeats her previous question, but again, there is no answer and there's no one else around. No one, except the ATM. Frowning, she steps closer and places a hand on the side of the machine.

LIZZIE

H-hello?

VOICE

Finally, someone who actually talks back! Hi there.

LIZZIE
Is anyone in there?

LIZZIE leans closer and knocks on the side of the machine.

VOICE
Ouch! Hey, watch it!

LIZZIE
(Gasps) I'm so sorry!

VOICE
(Chuckles) Just kidding! I'm an ATM machine, I can't feel
pain!

LIZZIE
O-oh, right. Why are you talking to me?

VOICE (now ATM)
You spoke to me first. And, well, no one talks to me. You're
the first person to really talk to me.

LIZZIE
I am?

ATM
Yup! I stand here all day, and people come up and press my
buttons, but no one says anything. They just take what they
want and leave.

LIZZIE
How rude!

ATM
Right? But hey, thanks for coming over to chat.

LIZZIE
You're, uh, welcome?

LIZZIE doesn't understand why the ATM is talking to her, but she's seven, so she doesn't question it.

ATM
So, you need money?

LIZZIE
Yeah! You see, there's this doll I want, and the store only has a limited number of them. I'm sure they'll all be gone by the end of day.

ATM
Well, like I said. I got money. Lots of it! How much do you need?

LIZZIE
(Thinks) I'm not sure. I mean, there's the doll, right, but then I gotta get her extra outfits, her accessories, and she has a pet poodle ...

ATM

Hmmm ... Well then, I got a bunch of money here, why don't I just give you all of it?

LIZZIE

All of it? Can you really do that?

ATM

Of course I can. Now, stand back!

LIZZIE

Stand back? Shouldn't you—

Lizzie lets out a squeal as the ATM spits out bills, sending them flying into the air.

LIZZIE

Holy shit! Oh no! That's a dollar in the swear jar.

LIZZIE's shout catches the attention of the customers, who all look at each other, confused, before rushing to grab the money flying out the ATM. MOM runs to Lizzie.

MOM

What's going on? Did you do this, Lizzie? I told you not to touch anything!

LIZZIE

I didn't! I mean, I did. But I didn't ask it to. Or I did. We were talking, and I said I needed money, and it said it had money ... but I didn't tell it to do that!

MOM pulls LIZZIE aside.

MOM
What do mean 'you were talking'? To whom?

LIZZIE
Me and the ATM. We were talking. It said it was bored standing around all day and I was the first person ever to really talk to it. (Sniffs as tears pour down her cheeks) A-am I in t-trouble?

MOM presses her lips together, then leans down to wipe her tears away.

MOM
No, honey. All right, let's go home. I think we need to call your Uncle Daric.

Mom had taken her back to their apartment where Uncle Daric was already waiting for them. Lizzie had always liked Uncle Daric because even though he was big and tall, he spoke so softly and gently. He asked her in a soothing tone to tell him everything that had happened. After that, he had brought her over to the TV and asked her if she could "talk to it." To her surprise, she was able to "talk" to the TV the way she did with the ATM, asking it to change channels and increase its volume. He did the same thing with their washing machine and security system.

Uncle Daric had then told her that she, like his children Cross and Astrid, was a hybrid—part Lycan, part witch. Like her cousins, she would not only eventually share her body with her wolf but had special powers. Hers allowed her to talk to machines. Technopathy, as he called it.

While she was born a witch, her mother, Selena Martin, didn't have active powers herself, so it was a surprise to them all. Uncle Daric had bound Lizzie's powers until she was old enough to learn how to control them and use them responsibly.

For the most part anyway.

See, there was that time she changed her best friend's grade in French from a D to a B+, but Lizzie reasoned that A) Tonya was going to pass anyway, all she did was help increase her GPA to qualify for that much-needed scholarship and B) Her teacher, Madame Grenouille, was a great big *putain* who made Tonya miserable all year and wanted to crush her hopes and dreams.

Bzzzttt!

The staticky crackling from her earpiece jolted Lizzie out of the memory, bringing her back to the present, where currently, she was sitting inside a cramped van parked in the tiny town of Lake Hope, Connecticut. The inside of said vehicle was packed with various computers and telecommunications devices, plus her two assistants—Ryerson and Cruz —typing away furiously at their terminals. It wasn't much— but it served an important purpose as the Lycans' central IT– communications hub for the battle with their enemies, the mages.

The final battle.

Tonight would decide their fate, humans and Lycans

alike. If they didn't succeed, it could be the end of the world as they knew it.

No pressure at all.

"Lizzie, status update?" came the voice from the comms. It was Lucas Anderson, Alpha of New York, her Lycan clan. Her inner wolf cowed down in deference, acknowledging his dominance.

"One sec, Primul." Looking up at the monitors, she placed her hands over the keyboard in front of her. "Show me where everyone is, Angie baby," she said to her main laptop, which she had named Angie.

Sure thing, Lizzie doll.

Machines did not only talk to her, but they also had unique personalities. Angie, for example, had a thick Brooklyn accent with an attitude to match. Whether that was something she made up or was how they were constructed, she wasn't sure. It had just always been that way.

All right, girlie, here we go! Angie chirped. *In ... 3 ... 2 ... 1 ...*

The monitor lit up as green blips on the screen appeared. The blinking lights signified the various teams of Lycans, along with their witch and human allies, converging on their target. Lizzie's gaze was drawn to one particular blip in the southwest quadrant of the map, moving into position toward the bottom of a hill.

There was nothing special about that blip that showed Team Alpha, led by her cousin, Cliff Forrest. It was one team out of many tonight, mobilizing to defeat their enemies.

Yup, nothing special at all.

At least, that's what she told herself.

Meanwhile, her animal's head perked up as she

continued to stare at it, and Lizzie's stomach did the most curious flip-flop.

"Lizzie?"

"Everyone's moving into position, Primul," she replied quickly.

"Excellent," the Alpha said. "Keep me posted if you see anything unusual."

Unusual?

They were about to launch a full-scale attack on their enemies who were trying to revive a centuries-dead master mage by kidnapping hundreds of people through magic. What other unusual thing Lizzie was supposed to keep an eye on, she wasn't sure, but she answered her Alpha with a quick, "Yep."

"Thanks, Lizzie. And you guys stay safe, okay?"

"Thank you, Primul. We will."

Turning back to her laptop, she tapped a few keys to check on their security and satellite positions. Of course, she didn't really need to use keyboards or a mouse or even her own voice to tell computers what to do as long as she was able to touch them physically. But she rather liked the clickety-clack sound the keys made and the way a machine responded to her commands. Lizzie found that even without her powers, she had a knack for working with computers. Her father taught her everything he knew about computers and hacking the old-fashioned way. After all, it was good to know the basics, and she loved the challenge of breaking into places she wasn't supposed to be in without using her powers.

Besides, the problem with machines was, the moment they figured out she could talk to them, they never shut up. The elevator back at HQ, for instance, couldn't take the hint that Lizzie was *not* interested in who was hooking up at the office after hours.

"Looks like the action's about to start," Cruz remarked, pointing to the screen. Most of the blips had stopped moving, which meant they were in position.

Lizzie's wolf scratched at her uneasily. Even though her wolf could easily crush a human with its jaws, she was not trained for fighting, nor did she have the stomach for it. Lizzie preferred to work in the background, using her magical and technical skills to help their agents in their missions. The last time she'd been in a fight—

A cold sweat broke over her brow at the memory of humungous arms around her, trapping her like a vice. A brief glimmer of hope as she escaped. The scrape of claws down her back. The heavy weight pressing her down ...

Her wolf shuddered and tucked its tail between its legs.

I know, she assured it. *But we're safe here.* The van was parked at the top of a hill, far away from where the battle would take place. Still, her wolf cowered in fear.

As a Lycan, Lizzie recovered quickly from the vicious ambush of a rival clan a few weeks ago. She acted as swiftly as she could, using her powers to quickly alert their team-mates, but not before she suffered injuries from that despicable Lycan from New Orleans, Jean-Baptiste. The pain of claws slashing through her flesh had been unbearable, like nothing she'd ever felt before.

Lizzie always thought that cliche of your life passing before your eyes during a near death experience silly. And truth be told, despite her own experience, she still thought it ridiculous. What had happened, in fact, was that in the moment before her rescue, as she felt the monstrous paws pressing her down and the rancid breath of the beast as her body weakened, the only thing Lizzie thought about were the things she never got to do and experience. Hiding behind her computers and tech all these years, Lizzie had realized she had never had the chance to do a lot of things.

Thankfully, Delacroix, another hybrid like herself, had rescued her and whisked her away to safety, albeit temporarily, before returning to the battle. It was while she waited for the fight to end and her body struggled to knit itself together, Lizzie had a lot of time to think about her life, all the way from the beginning, and what she missed out on. Things she didn't even know she wanted.

Then the strangest thing had happened.

The memory of it was hazy, but what she did remember was burned in her brain forever.

The buzz of electricity as a hand grazed along her skin.

A sensation of the earth falling away as strong arms lifted her up.

And the tantalizing scent she breathed in—vanilla, leather, burnt paper with a touch of sweet cherries—as she pressed her nose against warm skin comforted her and her wolf like nothing else ever could.

"Did you hear that?"

Once again, Lizzie was pulled back to the present. "Hear what?"

"Aren't you the Lycan here?" Cruz teased with a lopsided grin. Though part of the New York clan, she and Ryerson were both fully human, due to their parentage. Lycans could only produce full Lycan children with another of their kind.

There was one exception—True Mate children. If a Lycan mated with their human True Mate, they could have full-blooded Lycan offspring. Or in Lizzie's case, hybrid children because her parents were True Mates, destined by the fates to be together.

Lizzie snorted. "Oh, ha ha."

Cruz's eyebrows furrowed. "I swear, I heard something."

The hairs on the back of Lizzie's neck rose as she focused her enhanced hearing. She let out a gasp as she picked up the sound of footsteps. Several of them.

They found us!

Panic rose in her. The door was locked, but that wasn't going to stop anyone who was determined to get inside. And from the way the boots pounded on the ground as they drew closer, they sounded very determined indeed.

"Fuck!" Lizzie's heart began to pound like a drum.

Cruz paled. "They're coming for us, aren't they? How many?"

She blinked. "A dozen, at least."

Lizzie, your heartbeat is elevated and your blood pressure is increasing, her personal assistant–smartwatch, Eames, stated. *Shall I call for an ambulance?*

No! Definitely not. They couldn't risk alerting the—

"Mayday! Mayday!" Ryerson shouted into the mic connected to the main comms unit. "They've found us! They're right outside the van! Send help!"

"What the hell are you doing, Ryerson?" Lizzie scolded. "The teams are in position! We can't distract them now."

"Are you going to protect us?" Ryerson shot back. "I mean, I know you can change into your Lycan form, but if there's a dozen of them with guns ... well, we're toast."

Hope began to fade in her chest, and for a brief moment, Lizzie's life did flash before her eyes. Despite her first brush with death, she still hadn't done anything at all. She continued to hide behind the screen and keyboard. Never even acknowledging what she really, truly wanted in life.

The voices outside grew louder. The cocking of semi-automatic weapons made Lizzie's blood run cold.

"Open up," came the rough voice. "Or we'll pump you full of bullets."

And that last sliver of hope died.

Ignoring his inner wolf was as natural as breathing to Wyatt Creed.

Lycans, after all, had to keep their existence from the bigger world a secret. Who knew what humans would do it they found out people who turned into giant wolves lived among them? From the moment they were born, Lycans were sworn to secrecy.

Wyatt was only happy to comply. He always did, after all. Rules were kept in place to keep things orderly and civilized.

Tonight, however, Wyatt's control was being tested. But he couldn't blame his inner wolf for wanting to break free, because for the first time in his life, he would be counting on his beast to keep him alive.

Cliff Forrest held up a hand when they reached the bottom of the hill, and Wyatt and the three others behind him stopped. The hulking giant of a man—a former MMA champion— led their team as they closed in on their enemy's camp. Cliff then pointed to his ear, indicating that they were to wait for further instructions via the communications units.

Their Alpha, Lucas Anderson, took charge of the operations and gave out his commands from a nearby location.

Wyatt released a quiet breath and relaxed, at least for now. His wolf, however, remained tensed and ready.

At first, he thought his wolf would not be up for the battle. Then again, for the last few months, it seemed all he did was fight with his wolf. After letting Wyatt take the lead since it first manifested in his early teens, his wolf decided to start acting out.

Normally, his inner animal was quiet. In fact, some days, Wyatt could almost feel as if it wasn't there. He couldn't even remember the last time he shifted. It was as if they lived separate lives and his wolf lived in a completely different plane of existence.

A few months ago, however, it had been making its presence known, and rather vociferously too.

And when Wyatt attempted to leash back the animal, it only rebelled more.

Steady, he told his wolf. *You'll finally get what you want tonight.*

It let out a vicious sneer. Still, Wyatt could feel it relishing the thought of finally being let out to do some damage to their enemies. The pent-up energy nearly had him vibrating.

Savage. Feral. Vicious.

For now, Wyatt ignored the words ringing in his head. His existence, and those of his family and clan—and perhaps even the world—was at stake after all. He would be forgiven if, for just this once, he acted like an animal.

A pang of regret briefly made his gut clench, but Wyatt pushed it aside. Why should he have any regrets? He had a great career as VP of a multinational corporation, a penthouse apartment on the Upper East side, three vacation homes around the world, and anything and everything he wanted he could get with the snap of his fingers.

His wolf snorted in disagreement.

Oh, shut up.

Indeed, he had nothing to regret. If they were defeated tonight, there wouldn't even be anything to regret. There wouldn't be much left at all.

But they would not fail. Could not fail. Even his cynical side wouldn't allow him to think of defeat and the destruction of the world.

A loud piercing screech—feedback from the comms unit in his ear—had Wyatt and the rest of his team recoiling and flinching. Thankfully no one uttered a sound that could have alerted their enemies.

Cliff's face twisted in anger as he mouthed, *The fuck?*

"Mayday ..." came the crackly voice. "Found ... outside ... van ... help!"

Wyatt's blood ran cold. There was only one place where that call for help could have come from.

His wolf reacted immediately, desperate to tear out of him, but Wyatt held it back. The animal retaliated, but smart creature that it was, not with physical violence, rather, by sending him mental images.

Ripped up fuzzy pink sweater.

Open flesh.

Blood everywhere.

No!

Gritting his teeth, he pushed those images away. He'd worked so hard these last weeks trying not to think of them.

Even did everything he could to avoid having to remember what happened that day.

But as each second ticked by and only crackly static came from the comms, his anxiety swelled like a balloon. He and his team could only look at each other, paralyzed. The Alpha ordered them to stay in position until he mobilized them. None of them could leave or they could jeopardize the entire operation.

There was another burst of feedback from comms, followed by garbled voices, then a shrill, feminine scream.

"Get your hands off me!"

A fierce growl came from his wolf. Or perhaps it was from his own lips as Cliff turned to him, his eyes widening.

"Don't," Cliff warned in a low tone. "You can't—"

But Wyatt didn't hear the rest of it as he bolted away from the team. His wolf howled, and Wyatt felt its claws shredding its way out of his human body to take over.

Guided only by instinct, the giant brown wolf hurtled up the hill like it was being chased by the devil himself, its attention focused on its singular target. The black van was up ahead, the back door open as half a dozen armed men surrounded it. The wolf only pushed its muscles harder, leaping forward and ...

Wyatt couldn't quite remember what happened afterwards. Only that his wolf had overpowered him and he had no choice but to relinquish control. And perhaps, part of him wanted the animal to take over. To let it be the feral, vicious wolf it truly was. A thick, angry fog had taken over his mind, and he could not find his way out of it.

When Wyatt did emerge from that trance, the only thing he could perceive was pain. Sharp, throbbing pain all over his body. He could also sense that it was already light outside, but his eyelids were much too heavy, as was the rest of him. However, his body was beginning to knit itself back together, one of the advantages of being a Lycan.

A familiar scent drifted into his nostrils. Something comforting. Loving. Home.

Mom.

He tried to speak as a million thoughts ran through his brain. They didn't have a chance to speak before the battle. There had been no time. But now he wished they did, because he wanted to tell her so many things, things that were left unspoken over the years.

"... why don't you take my place for a bit...."

Soft hands lifted his head, and the lap he'd been resting on shifted. When his head came back down again, he knew it was someone else now.

If his body were capable of moving, he would have tensed as the delicious scent of strawberries swimming in champagne teased him. And his head was resting on top of something soft.

"... idiot was supposed to stay with Cliff ... take down six of them...."

His wolf sighed in pleasure. Wyatt didn't quite understand what else was going on around him, but, at least for now, he allowed himself to take in the sweet scent that had been haunting him for months. This time, it was him who was injured, and him being comforted by her softness and warmth.

Her breath sent a tingle down his spine as she moved close to whisper in his ear.

"If you die today, I'm going to hack into your credit card

and order ball gags and gimp suits and have them sent to your office. Or parents' house."

Despite her threats, her voice was the sweetest sound in the world.

She was safe and alive.

Chapter One

Present time ...

"**W**asn't that performance just divine, Wyatt?"
Wyatt's head snapped back to the woman beside him. He'd been thinking about his to-do list for the next day when the sound of applause and cheers brought him back. Where was he?

Ah, right.

Lincoln Center. New York City Ballet's performance of Swan Lake. Front Row, sitting beside his date and companion for the evening, Sandra Collingsworth. They'd met at a party a few months ago when he was in London, but he had to leave for Switzerland later that evening. So when a business trip brought her to New York, she contacted him and asked if he wanted to go out. Her dates in the city happened to coincide with this charity performance, so he had brought her as his plus one.

"Absolutely," he agreed with a nod and clapped his hands together as the dancers took their bows.

"Thank you for inviting me. These seats are amazing."

He had certainly paid enough for them, so he hoped they were amazing. "I'm glad you came."

His wolf taunted him at the words.

"I need to thank your grandmother for giving me your number next time I see her."

Of course Grandmama would give his number to Sandra. In fact, now that he thought about it, perhaps it was no mere coincidence that she had been there at the party at Oxley Park. After all, Sandra Collingsworth was exactly the type of woman Fiona Hastings, Lady Oxley would approve of—cultured, rich, and the granddaughter of an Earl.

"How is she, by the way?" he asked.

"Doing well," she replied with a chuckle. "But why ask me that? She's your grandmother, surely, you've seen or spoken to her recently?"

Wyatt straightened his shoulders. "I'm afraid I haven't been back to England since we met. I've been busy."

"Of course. Your promotion," she replied with a nod. "Congratulations, by the way. CEO of Creed Security. Lady Oxley must be so proud of you."

If you only knew. He bit his tongue. "I believe they're having a small cocktail reception for patrons," he said, quickly changing the subject. "We can meet the director, the dancers, and producers."

"Wonderful. I'd love that."

Wyatt stood up, and Sandra took the hand he offered. As they walked toward the exit, he couldn't help but feel eyes on him as they strolled by.

Truly, he should be used to it by now. Ever since that night, his entire world changed, and people looked at him differently.

After all, everyone here knew *what* he really was.

Wolf.

Monster.

Savage.

While they had saved the world and prevailed over their enemies, the Lycans had been exposed, and now the whole world knew of their existence. The whispers around him might as well have been shouts; unfortunately, enhanced hearing was one of the "gifts" of being a Lycan.

"That's him...."

"A Supernatural...."

"... turn into animals...."

But he was adept at ignoring them. And no one would dare say anything to his face. Truth be told, his inner wolf rather liked the idea of being feared.

"Good evening, Mr. Creed," the distinguished-looking usher greeted as they approached the door that led to the function room where the cocktail party was taking place. "You can go right inside."

Well-dressed men and women milled about, sipping champagne brought to them by waiters in tuxes and tails, right under glittering crystal chandeliers that probably cost more than the average person made in a year. Every eye in the room turned to them as they passed by. Here, no one cared that he was a Lycan. To them, he was a powerful man— a billionaire CEO who could affect the lives of thousands with a wave of his hand.

This was where he belonged—among the beautiful,

cultured, and rich people, with a gorgeous woman on his arm and everyone looking at him with envy.

Well, at least a few months ago, that's what he would have thought.

Now he didn't know where he belonged anymore.

His wolf whined, trying to catch his attention.

And as he usually did, he paid it no heed and instead walked over to the famous Hollywood actor standing by the bar so he could introduce Sandra to him.

However, there were certain things he could not ignore.

Like how a flash of red hair from the corner of his eye made his head turn involuntarily.

Or how the glass of champagne in his hand reminded him of that familiar, delicious scent.

Or how the blue banners strewn across the ceiling was the exact shade of *her* eyes.

No, such things led to dangerous thoughts, and he shut it—and his wolf—down quickly.

For the rest of the night, he went through the motions, talking with the right people, telling them the stories they wanted to hear, laughing at their stupid jokes, but his mind did not absorb any of the goings-on. By the end of the evening, the only emotion he felt was relief when he finally climbed into his limousine.

"I had a great time, Wyatt," Sandra said as she slid in next to him. "So, how about a nightcap at my hotel?" She leaned toward him invitingly,

Wyatt knew what kind of nightcap she was talking about and what answer he should give her. His wolf, however, begged to differ. "To the Plaza," he told his driver.

The hotel was not that far from the Lincoln Center, and

soon they were pulling up to the famous Plaza Hotel driveway in front of Central Park. The door opened, and Sandra stepped outside.

"Wyatt?" Her brows furrowed as she looked back at him from the sidewalk where she had alighted.

"Actually," he began. "I just remembered I have to go back to the office."

Her lips pursed. "Now?"

"Yes."

Sandra's pretty face flashed surprise and anger for a moment before she stood up straight. "Fine." She flipped her hair over her shoulder. "Just so you know, I don't give second chances."

"Noted. Good night, Sandra." Wyatt nodded to his driver, Morrison, who closed the door. With his enhanced hearing he heard Sandra let out a miffed *harrumph* as she muttered under her breath, *you're making a big mistake.*

Somehow, he doubted that.

"Back to HQ, Mr. Creed?" Morrison asked.

A beat passed before he answered. "No."

"Home then?"

The thought of entering his empty penthouse apartment did not sit well with him. "One moment." Fishing his phone out of his pocket, he tapped on the envelope icon. After scrolling through the dozens of messages, he found his brother's last text from a few days ago—it was a selfie of him at some wild party, surrounded by bikini-clad women.

Hop on your jet and join me in Capri, bro.

Can't. Too busy.

> All right. If the mountain won't come to
> Muhammed ... I'll be home on Tuesday.

Wyatt smiled to himself. Despite them being complete opposites, he and Bastian remained close over the years, though that was mostly because of his brother's tenacious nature. In the years that Wyatt lived in England, he had all but forgotten about the life he left in America, but Bastian refused to stay away.

He truly loved his younger brother and held no grudge against him, and was actually proud of his accomplishments. It had been weeks since they had seen each other, as Bastian often traveled around the world as CEO of his own tech company, one that he built from scratch without help from anyone else. While it was usually Bastian pestering him to hang out, Wyatt found himself seeking his brother's grounding presence.

Are you home yet? he texted back. A minute passed and there was no reply, not even the small dots at the bottom of the screen to indicate he was typing. Bastian was forever glued to his phone which meant he had no reception and was probably still in the air. He contemplated waiting for the next day, but then they would both be busy with meetings and work. Besides, Bastian wouldn't mind if he showed up unannounced at his home.

"Morrison, could you head over to my brother's place, please?"

"Right away, sir."

Wyatt settled back as the limo made its way to Hudson Yards, where the younger Creed kept a luxurious condominium with a magnificent view of the river. It was brand new, shiny, and state-of-the art—everything Bastian loved and Wyatt abhorred. Wyatt's penthouse was on top of a turn of the century building, with antique furnishings from all over Europe, paintings of English landscapes, and plush Persian carpets, while Bastian's condo was all leather and glass and steel. The last time Wyatt was there he'd had this garish pink and neon green abomination of a painting on one wall.

But, one thing Wyatt appreciated was that Bastian had given him his own digital key on his phone so he could access the place anytime he wanted. Wyatt had never had to use it before tonight, but he figured it would be easier to wait for Bastian at his condo than sit at home twiddling his thumbs.

When the door to his limo opened, Wyatt stepped out. "I might be a while, Morrison," he told the driver. "You can head home. I'll find my own way back." Knowing Bastian anyway, they might be up all night drinking and talking. Thankfully, as Lycans, they didn't need much sleep, nor did they get drunk or have hangovers.

The automatic glass doors made a soft swoosh as soon as Wyatt stepped in front of it. As he walked by the front desk, he waved away the uniformed man behind it with a flash of his digital key. Everything was automated with the key, and the sleek, mirrored elevators brought him to the correct floor without Wyatt touching even one button. When he reached Bastian's floor, he strode over to the lone door across the hallway. Before he could even raise his phone to the sensor, he heard the sound of footsteps and the whirring of the locks as they disengaged.

Huh. Funny that Bastian didn't reply to my message if he'd been home all this time.

When the door opened, however, his brother wasn't on the other side.

Every nerve ending in his body sizzled as the red-headed female appeared before him, and his wolf yelped in excitement as it recognized her delicious strawberries and champagne scent.

"Hey, Bastian, you're home—oh, it's you." Arctic-blue eyes widened before blinking up at him, her plump pink lips parting. "W-what are you doing here?"

"Lizzie."

It felt like forever since he last said her name aloud. As if he'd been afraid to say it and hear it from his own lips, lest he conjure her up like some specter.

And now, here she was, in the flesh. The woman who'd been haunting his every dream and waking moment for the last few months. A familiar ache formed low in his stomach, as a feverish desire lit up inside him

The arousal, however, was quickly replaced with rage when he realized she was wearing one of her signature cartoon T-shirts and a pair of men's boxers.

Chapter Two

Nothing challenged Lizzie more than a puzzle.

There was no problem she couldn't figure out, no code she couldn't break, no firewall she couldn't breach.

But Wyatt Creed was more than a puzzle. He was a mystery, rolled up in a conundrum, then deep fried in confusion. Topped off with a dash of *what-the-fuck, man.*

Her inner wolf, however, always reacted the same way the moment he was anywhere within two feet of them. Its ears would perk up and stand at attention, then it went completely still as if waiting for ... something.

Even putting aside her animal's strange behavior, she didn't know what to think about Wyatt Creed, how to solve him, and how to figure out how he worked or break down his defenses. And more often than not, she was left confused.

Take this instance, for example.

Said man shows up unannounced, in the middle of the night, at his brother's apartment. Lizzie didn't even know he had a key, but here he was, with a strange look on his face.

Like he was keeping something bottled up inside that was ready to explode, a quiet rage brewing behind those light hazel eyes. His large hands were balled up into fists, and his shoulders were so tense, she could practically hear the seams of his expensive tux ripping.

Hope he has a good tailor.

"I—"

"You—"

They spoke at the same time, causing them both to stop and lock gazes for what seemed like an eternity. An unfamiliar sensation gripped Lizzie, rooting her to the spot and making it difficult to turn away from those mesmerizing eyes.

Before either could say anything else, a familiar voice from the hallway made them both start.

"Wyatt? What are you doing here?" Bastian Creed's face lit up with a bright smile as he came up behind Wyatt. "Bro! I knew you missed me, but not this much." He dropped his overnight bag on the floor and pulled him in for a hug. "Glad to see you."

Wyatt remained stiff and did not return the hug. "Sorry. I thought you'd be alone." His voice sounded taut, like a string ready to snap at any moment.

"Alone? Yeah, I'm—" Bastian's gaze darted from Lizzie then back to his brother, then the corner of his mouth quirked up. "Hey babe, what's up?"

Babe? He'd never called her that before. "Don't you 'what's up' me, Bastian Creed." She crossed her arms under her breasts. "You're late."

"Sorry, about that," he said with a grin. "I promise I'll make it up to you."

Lizzie rolled her eyes. "You better, mister."

"How's my baby, by the way?"

Wyatt let out a strangled noise before clearing his throat. "I hate to interrupt your evening plans, so I'll be on my way." Pivoting on his heel, he marched off without another word and headed into the elevator.

"Bro!" Bastian called, but it was too late as the soft ping indicated the doors had closed. He clucked his tongue and glanced back at Lizzie, a sly look on his face. "What did he say when you answered the door? Did you tell him anything?"

"Didn't even get the chance to. He arrived seconds before you did." She frowned. "Do you think he was upset about something?"

Bastian threw his head back and laughed. "I would say so." His dark brows knitted together. "You ... didn't notice anything else about him?"

She shrugged. "Should I?"

He muttered something under his breath that sounded like *so oblivious*. "Never mind." He nodded toward the inside of his apartment. "C'mon, I've missed my baby, and I can't wait to cuddle her."

Lizzie grinned. "And she's missed you too." Stepping aside, she let Bastian in, who, predictably, dashed over to the metal playpen set up in the corner of the massive living room. Bending over, he picked up the ball of fur curled up in the corner.

"Hello, baby girl," he greeted. "Did you miss Daddy? I missed you, Jessica baby."

Lizzie couldn't help but smile at the sight of the tall, hulking bearded and tattooed tech CEO whose heart was captured by this tiny creature.

And an ugly one at that.

To say the dog was unattractive was an understatement. The mutt was about the size of a football, with black and brown fur that stuck out like weeds no matter how much Lizzie brushed her. The dog's severe underbite should have made it look mean, except the little fur ball was perky and cheerful all the time. Currently, it was wiggling in happiness as Bastian rained kisses on its face. Lizzie had no idea where Bastian got Jessica, but it was obvious he was smitten with her. She was perhaps the first female who'd ever held the notorious playboy CEO's undivided attention.

After more licks and kisses, Bastian plopped down on the couch with Jessica on his lap. The dog was on its back, its tongue sticking out the side of its mouth in ecstasy as her master indulged her in belly rubs.

"Thanks again for watching her," Bastian said. "I'm working on getting her shots and everything so she can travel with me."

"Of course, no prob." Lizzie motioned to the boxers she was wearing. "She had an accident so I had to change out of my skirt, I hope you don't mind I borrowed these."

"Oops, sorry about that. She was probably excited to see you. But yeah, of course. Mi casa is su casa, especially when you're doing me a big favor." He gave Jessica a kiss on belly. "Did you have a good time with Auntie Lizzie, baby?" The mutt gave an excited yip. "Did she give you much trouble?"

"Nah. Except for the accident, she was a sweetheart as always."

He flashed her a grin that would have probably sent most hearts a flutter. "You're a doll, babe."

With a roll of her eyes, she sat down next to him. "What's with this 'babe' business anyway?"

He gave another bark of laughter. "Oh nothing. Just something I like to say to friends. I'll stop if you don't like it."

Lizzie wasn't sure exactly how she and Bastian became friends and how she ended up being his dog sitter. She was older than him by a few years, and he was technically her boss's son and a client, but here they were. She doubted anyone could say no to the persuasive and smooth-talking Sebastian Creed Junior.

"Hey now, what's this?" Reaching over to the side table, Bastian picked up a glossy magazine from a pile. "Is that—"

Mortification flooded Lizzie's cheeks with warmth. "That's nothing!" She lunged forward in an attempt to snatch the magazine from Bastian, but he was too quick. With Jessica under his arm, he shot up away from her.

"'Maxim Silver,'" he read aloud from the cover. "'An interview with the Financial Disrupter.'" Glancing over at the remaining stack, he frowned. "'The Silver Fox: Tech's Newest Man About Town.'" Sliding that one away, he picked up the last one: *Up Close Weekly*. "'Top 10 Hottest Bachelor CEOs'—Oh, did this one come out already? My publicist didn't say anything. Did my ranking—hey!"

This time, Lizzie managed to grab the magazine from him. "Get your own copy." She held the magazine to her chest like a shield.

"Are you—oh my God, Lizzie, is this the geeky version of *Playgirl*?" Bastian said with a chuckle. "Are you turned on by reading about blockchain and cloud computing?"

She wasn't sure how, but her cheeks were now the surface temperature of Mars. "N-no!"

Bastian's eyes darted from the magazine in his hand, to the one on the table, and finally to the one she clutched to her body. Being a smart man, he quickly figured out what they all had in common. "What the—Maxim Silver? Really?"

"I—" With a defeated sigh, she sunk down to the plush leather couch. "It's not what you think."

"Really? Because my brain can get really wild."

She looked up at him sheepishly. "Okay, so maybe it is what you think." But how was she supposed to explain to him her deeply embarrassing—and very much unrequited—infatuation with Maxim Silver, CEO of Silver Securities Tech Worldwide?

"This guy?" Bastian asked, incredulous. "Him?"

"Argh!" She reclined back on the couch dramatically. "You don't understand."

"Then tell me more. I'm your friend, right?"

Glancing back at the first magazine cover, Lizzie found herself mesmerized by Maxim Silver's dark blue eyes and that dazzling smile. And his strong jaw, straight nose, and tousled black hair with that touch of silver at the temples.

And he was even hotter in person.

"Arch brought him in as a potential client and he's been coming into Lone Wolf for the past couple of days." Lizzie began. "Might hire us for a job."

Bastian's lips pulled back into a thin line. "Did he flirt with you? Try anything inappropriate?"

She blew out a breath. "I wish. He's never even spoken directly to me. Being a potential VIP client, he's only met with Uncle Killian or Dad. I don't even know what kind of project they're working on."

"You've never had a conversation with him?"

She shook her head.

Well, actually, Maxim Silver did speak to her once. It was last Wednesday, at one fifty-two in the afternoon, just outside her father's office. Not knowing he was in there, she was about to barge in when he came out at the same time. She'd been so stunned by the fact that she was inches away from Maxim Silver that she didn't even realize he'd mistaken her for one of the secretaries and given her his coffee order.

"And yet, you have this major crush on him?"

"Hey, you're one to talk," she shot back. "Tell me the name of the last supermodel you banged."

He held a hand up defensively. "That's different."

"Because you're a guy?"

"No." He sat back down and put Jessica between them. "That was sex. I tell women I sleep with from the beginning that that's all it's going to be. But"—the furrow between his eyebrows deepened—"I think this is more than just sex."

Lizzie didn't know why, but that seemed to worry Bastian. "I ... maybe. Wait—why do you think that?"

"Because, Lizzie, no offense, but you're not a casual sex kind of girl."

Bastian was not wrong.

Actually, Lizzie was not any kind of sex girl at all.

Yes, at thirty-two years of age, Elizabeth Eowyn Martin was still in possession of her dreaded *V* card.

How did this happen?

She was a genius, they'd said.

Turned out, even with her powers bound, Lizzie had a natural talent and affinity for computers, math, and science. By the time she was thirteen and her powers were unbound, she was skipping grades so fast, it had been easier to home-school her. Well, that and the fact that she literally spoke with computers, not to mention, her Lycan side was manifesting, puberty had been a hot mess.

That meant she never went to school with kids her own age, never had the high school or college experience. In fact, she only made it through one semester of college when she was fifteen before she quit and started working for Lone Wolf. She loved the challenge and being able to work on her own with just her computers, and she was content and happy with her life the way it was.

Or at least she thought she was.

It seemed while she hid behind her laptop and machines, life just went on and left her behind. Two close brushes with death made her re-examine her life. Like what she really wanted. And while she was doing that, Maxim Silver walked into her life—er, rather, the office—looking so incredibly handsome and irresistible. When she did her research on him, well, the man seemed tailor-made just for her.

Maxim Silver. Forty years of age. Graduated with honors from MIT at the age of twenty-two. Sold his first piece of software at twenty-five, then started his own tech company with the profit. Now he ran one of the largest FinTech companies in the world and was worth millions of dollars. He was also single, never married, though his interviews—usually puff pieces for women's magazines and websites—indicated he was searching for the one.

I could be that one.

"Damn it!"

"Huh?" While she was daydreaming about Maxim, Bastian had snatched *Up Close Weekly* from her arms and was now rifling through it. "Hey, I haven't even opened that."

"Tragedy," he declared in a dramatic tone of voice.

"What is?"

"This." He spread out the glossy magazine between them and pointed to the open page. "Not only am I ranked number seven again this year, but now I have to share the honor with my brother?"

Sure, enough, next to Bastian's bare chested, tattooed photo was Wyatt, looking all serious in his expensive three-piece suit.

Lizzie's mouth went dry. Hazel eyes so light they were almost yellow bore straight into her soul, sending a strange zing all the way to her lower belly. Again, Wyatt was making her all confused. Why couldn't he be more like a computer, so she could easily figure him out?

"Like what you see?" Bastian teased.

"Ha! You've showed off more than that on your Instagram," she said wryly. With a deep sigh, she stood up. "I should get going. Jessica's been fed and walked, so she's ready for bed."

He waved the copy of *Up Close Weekly* at her. "Don't you want your magazines?"

"Nah, I can get digital copies."

Bastian settled Jessica on top of a pillow, then followed Lizzie as she picked up her duffel bag and headed toward the door. "Hey, you know that magazine is having some kind of party the day after tomorrow. I wasn't gonna go, but now I'm thinking ... you wanna come with me?"

She spun around to face him. "On a date?"

"Not 'a date,'" he clarified. "As my plus one. Strictly platonic."

"Why me?" She eyed him suspiciously. "Don't you have

an address book full of celebrities and supermodels who come running at a snap of your fingers?"

He chuckled. "Yeah, but you're a hell of a lot more fun than they are. Besides, you know who else is coming?" He nodded back at the magazines sprawled on the couch around a snoozing Jessica.

"Who—oh!" *Maxim Silver*. "Do you think he's going to show up?"

"He's number one on that list, of course he will," he assured her.

That means she'd be able to talk to him outside the office. Maybe even flirt with him a little. "Oh ... yeah, count me in."

He grinned at her. "You have something to wear, right?"

"Duh, of course I do."

"Like, a dress. A real one."

"Aww, fuck off, Creed." She swatted him playfully on the shoulder. Actually, she only had one dress that would be appropriate for a party, one she usually wore to formal events. No one paid attention to her anyway, and if anyone noticed she wore the same dress twice, they never said anything. "I won't embarrass you, okay?"

"Great, I'll send you more details tomorrow."

"Awesome. Well, I gotta get home."

"Do you want my driver to bring you home?"

"Nah, I'll call a car."

"All right, thanks again."

As the door closed behind her, Lizzie heard the electronic lock say, *Bye Lizzie! Come back and visit, ya hear?*

"Will do," she replied with a wave. "Eames?"

Yes, Lizzie?

To Lizzie, her smartwatch/personal assistant sounded a

lot like a British butler, which was why she named him Eames. "I'd like to go home now. Could you call me a car, please?"

Booking now ... Your car is five minutes away, black Honda Civic. License plate NA456T and your driver is Gene H. Gene has an average rating of four-point-oh, and other riders have complimented him on his conversational skills and clean interiors.

"Sounds great, Eames." Lizzie slung her duffel bag over her shoulder and stepped into the elevator when it arrived. It greeted her with a cheerful, *Evening, Lizzie!* as she stepped inside, to which she replied with a muted hello. Elevators were always chatty and this one was no exception. As it always did, it talked her ear off, but thankfully, the ride down was quick. After a curt goodbye, she made her way across the sleek lobby and straight outside to where her rideshare car was already waiting.

"You Gene?" she asked the driver as she opened the door.

"Yeah. Lizzie? Headed to the Lower East Side?"

"Yup." Tossing her duffel in first, she scooted inside.

Gene put the car into gear and they were off. As Lizzie settled in, he glanced back at her. "Do you mind if I turn up the radio? I've been waiting for this segment for a while."

"No, go ahead."

"Great!" He turned the volume knob up. "I love this guy! And listening to him makes these late nights driving around more bearable."

Thanks again to our sponsors, Midtown Mattresses! The voice that burst through the speakers was male. *And welcome back to the Larry Eastman Show. I'm your host, Larry Eastman.*

Lizzie groaned inwardly. *Oh God, not this idiot!*

Larry Eastman was a national radio jockey well known for his controversial views and targeting of certain groups of people he didn't like. Or maybe it wasn't that he didn't like these groups, but his listener base didn't, and Eastman loved nothing more than to rile them up for ratings.

So, as I said before the break, when we come back, I wanted to talk about the Supernaturals.

Unfortunately, his latest target were Lycans and witches.

And here we go. Lizzie bit her lip to stop from speaking out. *What a terrible time to have ears.*

If you recall, folks, Larry began, *a couple of months ago, the supernatural beings—people who turn into giant wolves, as well as witches and warlocks with magical powers—revealed themselves to the rest of the world after hiding for hundreds of years.* He scoffed. *If you ask me, they should have stayed hidden. I mean, how could we humans possibly feel safe now that we know that they're everywhere?*

"Yeah. Uh-huh." Gene's head bobbed up and down with vigor. "Can you believe it? All this time, they've been living like us. I mean, I got kids at school, what if one of them attacks them?"

Great conversation skills, my ass. Gene was definitely getting a one-star rating.

"Aren't you scared of them?"

"Mm-hmm," she hummed noncommittally.

As Larry Eastman continued with his hate-filled and ignorant tirade, Lizzie did her best to tune him out. Thankfully, at this time there was no traffic, and they reached her apartment building in no time.

"We're here, Lizzie." Gene announced.

Lizzie mumbled her thanks as she bolted out of the car and made her way to her sixth-floor walkup. Dropping her bag on the floor as she entered, she trudged toward her bedroom.

As she prepared for sleep, her thoughts kept straying to Larry Eastman. His voice and opinion were just one among the seven billion in the world, but, unfortunately, many humans agreed with him.

The reaction among the Lycan and magical community was just as mixed. There were many who hadn't wanted to be outed, and Lizzie couldn't blame them as none of them had a choice.

In order to revive their master, the mages had kidnapped three hundred humans to use in their ritual and kept them in a trance-like state. Immediately after the Lycan forces defeated the mages, the humans regained control of their senses. Confused, they all started taking videos, posted on social media, and of course, called the authorities when they realized they'd been abducted.

That led to a giant shit show and a Congressional hearing, which frankly everyone thought had shut down any protests, and everyone lived in harmony forever and ever.

At least in the fairy-tale, idealized version, that's what would have happened, but of course, that was far from what occurred and was continuing to occur to this day. If history taught Lizzie anything, it was that humans always hated what they perceived as different from them—"others" and the "them" who were "not like us."

If she were truly honest with herself, however, Lizzie didn't mind that the larger world now knew their secret. Frankly, keeping her true identity secret—both her Lycan and witch side—had always bothered her. Ever since the humans had found out about their true natures, it was as if a big weight had been lifted off her shoulders.

And now that she no longer had to hide who and what she was, she could focus on the things she wanted. Her life had seemingly passed by, but she was ready to live it. And perhaps Maxim Silver was what she needed right now.

The following day, Lizzie got up and dressed in her usual outfit—a short plaid wool skirt, black knee-high boots, and a T-shirt that said, 'Sarcasm is my love language'—then headed out to the offices of Lone Wolf Investigations and Security in Midtown. To her surprise, just as she entered through the glass doors, her own father was walking out.

"Oh good, you're here," Quinn Martin greeted his daughter. Father and daughter shared the same arctic-blue eyes, but Lizzie resembled her mother more, with her red hair and curvy frame.

She nodded at the laptop bag in his hand. "Where're you off to in such a hurry, Pops?"

"Fenrir," he replied tensely. "There's been an attempted breach of their systems."

Lizzie tsked. "Another one?"

Ever since the Lycans were outed and Lucas Anderson was revealed as the Alpha of New York, his company, Fenrir Corporation, had been heavily targeted by various hackers and possibly enemy states. Lone Wolf, particularly Lizzie and her father, had been monitoring the situation, ready to pounce into action if needed. "Should I come along?"

"Nah, they didn't get very far, but I still need to check it out. But I do need you to go to Creed to check on their firewall and make sure no one's tried to get through it."

Fenrir Corp and Creed Security were Lone Wolf's biggest clients. Actually, Lone Wolf was a subsidiary of Creed Security, which made the big kahuna himself, AKA Sebastian Creed AKA the dragon shifter, her main boss. And because of the nature of her powers and the possibility of it being used for nefarious purposes by outsiders, Lizzie was only ever allowed to work on the Creed and Fenrir accounts. The exact nature of her particular set of magical skills was on a need-to-know basis only.

"I'll head over there now." Turning around, she marched back to the elevators.

"Wearing that?" Quinn looked her up and down, then shook his head. "Why can't you ever dress normally? This is a professional place of business, you know."

She stuck her tongue out at him. "No one cares what I look like, least of all the dragon." In the past, Mr. Creed had been so impressed with her work and skills, he'd mentioned it was a shame she couldn't take work for his clients. "I'm the best in the biz, after all."

And just for the heck of it—or maybe to get back at him for making fun of her outfit—she instructed the elevator to leave before her father could step in.

"Sebastian? But he's not the—hey, what the—"

"You snooze, you lose, old man!" She flashed him a smug grin as she waved from behind the closing doors.

After taking a rideshare downtown—no chatty drivers or bigoted radio hosts, thank goodness—Lizzie strode into the Creed Securities headquarters. She didn't bother to stop by the reception desks as all she had to do was touch the security gates and they were only too happy to let her in. Breezing straight into the executive elevators, the car whisked her all the way to the top floor.

It was early, not even eight, so the CEO's floor was still dark and quiet. The lights flickered on as she stepped out of the elevator and made her way to Creed's office.

Lizzie had done these checks as well as the regular maintenance of the security systems numerous times before over the years, and Mr. Creed always preferred she start by checking his work computer first before she went to the IT department. *I can't trust anyone but you, Lizzie*, he always said.

Humming to herself, she let herself into the humungous corner office with glass walls that revealed a view of the Hudson River and New Jersey that never failed to impress her.

As she took in a quick breath, the skin at the back of her neck prickled. There was something different about the office today, she just couldn't figure out what. Something very familiar. Her wolf, too, sensed something, as it raised its head and took a deep sniff. It wasn't panicking nor did it try to warn her about any sort of danger, so she shrugged and went around the large mahogany table by the window and booted up the computer.

Placing her hand on the monitor, she said, "Hey there, what's shaking?"

Whoa! You can talk! And you can hear me? the confused-sounding computer replied. *Cool.*

"Sure can," she replied with a chuckle. "And you're new

around here, aren't you?" Hmmm, no one told her they had replaced Mr. Creed's computer.

Not exactly. I used to be a couple of floors down until they moved me up here.

"Oh really?" Lizzie took her laptop out of her backpack. "That's cool. Just so you know, I'm here to make sure you haven't been breached."

B-breached? The computer sounded worried.

"Yeah, you can't be too careful these days. Anyway, let me introduce you to a good friend of mine. Her name's Angie. She's can be a little abrasive and forward, but she'll take good care of you."

Pushing the brand-new leather chair aside, Lizzie crawled under the chair so she could hook up Angie to the new computer. The CPU itself looked like the standard-issued Creed Securities PC unit, so she was at least familiar with all the ports. She was reaching behind it to plug in her cable when a voice made her start, making her bang her head on the underside of the table.

"Who the hell is in here?"

"Yeow!"

Quickly, she backed out from the under the desk, still on her hands and knees, her gaze fixing on a pair of expensive leather shoes. Her head snapped up and crashed into the hazel eyes of Wyatt Creed.

What the heck was he doing here?

Chapter Three

What the fuck was she doing here?

For a moment, Wyatt thought he'd been dreaming. Or maybe lack of sleep made him hallucinate. Because finding Lizzie on her hands and knees under his desk was the last thing he expected to find this morning. In fact, after his terrible, sleepless evening, he had hoped to never see her again.

His inner wolf, however, did not agree. It perked up just being near her, whining with happiness while still being pissed at him at the same time for leaving so quickly last night.

Damn wolf.

Shock, anger, and disbelief all jumbled together in his mind at what he'd witnessed the previous evening. But there was no denying it—Bastian and Lizzie were together. What they were exactly, he didn't know, but he did know his brother. Bastian had a one night only policy when it came to women and never brought them to his home. It was always at her place or an anonymous hotel. He had also never introduced a woman he was seeing or sleeping with to Wyatt or anyone in their family, nor did he eye any female even remotely related to their clan. Yet the scene he walked in on was obviously domestic.

In any case, he didn't bother staying to find out. No, he had to get out of there before he did something stupid.

Wyatt walked all the way home, hoping that the exercise would ease his mind. But if anything, his simmering anger had turned into a full-blown rage by the time he entered his apartment. Images of Bastian and Lizzie together tortured him, his chest gripped by a harsh pain that made it difficult to breathe. He sat on his couch in a daze, not moving, sipping on a glass of the finest single malt scotch whiskey in his collection. Before he knew it, the sun was peeking into his windows, and the bottle lay empty next to him.

Bastian and Lizzie.

Lizzie and Bastian.

"Hello?" Lizzie jumped up and down in front of him, waving her hand in his face. "Are you okay?"

"I'm fine," he said through gritted teeth, though he couldn't ignore how her full breasts bounced underneath the ridiculous shirt she wore. "What are you doing here?"

"There was a security breach at Fenrir."

"What?" For a moment, Wyatt forgot all about his stupid brother. "Did they get into our systems here too?" Now it made sense why she was here.

"No, but the office sent me to make sure you're all secure." She jerked a thumb at his desk.

"But why are you here? Shouldn't you head down to IT?" On second thought, that might not be a good idea, considering how she was dressed. Those horny geeks would probably stare at her until their eyes fell out of their sockets.

"Yeah, but I always check the boss's computer first. CEO's orders."

Wyatt crossed his arms over his chest. "I am the boss," he said. "I'm the new CEO of Creed Security," he reminded her.

"Really? Since when?" She didn't sound impressed at all. In fact, from the way she reacted, it was as if he'd told her something mundane, like the sky was blue or it was raining outside.

"Since the Congressional hearings."

"Oh, right," she said with cluck of her tongue and a point of a finger. "Awesome, congrats then. Do you still want me to check on your computer?"

"Go ahead."

"Great!" Bending down, she crawled back under the desk.

Wyatt stifled a groan as her short plaid skirt flipped invitingly. He quickly looked away and raked his fingers through his hair.

Christ, this was going to be a long morning.

Before he could do or say anything else, Lizzie said something incomprehensible from under the desk.

"What was that?"

She didn't answer but continued chattering on, and like the idiot he was, Wyatt remained standing over her. Minutes later, her head popped out.

"All done," she declared cheerfully, then crawled out again, thankfully this time, facing forward. "Everything looks good, no breach here. Firewalls are up and running, though I recommend we update a few protocols to increase security. I was talking to your computer, and he said—"

"I beg your pardon? Who were you talking to?"

"Your computer," she stated.

Ah, right. Lizzie was a hybrid and could talk to computers, though he'd never actually seen her use her powers, even when they worked together in the Guardian Initiative. "You actually talk to them?"

"Yup," she said, popping the *p* at the end.

"And they talk back."

She nodded, shoved a hand into the pocket of her skirt, and produced a lollipop. Unwrapping it, she stuck the bright red end in her mouth, her pink tongue briefly peeking out between her lips.

Wyatt strangled a groan in his throat.

"Everything is peachy keen up here." After packing up her laptop, she slung her backpack over a shoulder. "Unless there's anything else, I'll head down to IT."

"No, you can go."

She gave him a thumbs-up. "Right-o!"

When she turned on her heel and pivoted, he found himself yelling out, "Wait!"

She did an about-face. "Yes? What is it?"

"I ..." His mouth went completely dry, unsure what to say.

For fuck's sake, Wyatt, get a grip.

He was an adult. In fact, they were all adults. Him, Bastian, and Lizzie, and they all damned well better start acting like adults. Clearing his throat, he began with, "I just wanted to say ... you and Bastian ... congratulations?"

Her jaw dropped, the lollipop dangling from her lips. "What now?"

"I mean ... I'm happy for you both. Er, support whatever it is ..." *Fuck, fuck, fuck.* He scrubbed a hand down his face. *Fratricide was a sin, fratricide was a sin,* he repeated like a mantra. *And also, a crime.* "Look, you two are obviously a good match and I"—he swallowed what seemed like a handful of nails scraping down his gullet—"support the two of you."

Lizzie remained still for a moment, her eyebrows going all the way up to her hairline. "You ... support us?"

"Yeah. Your relationship, I mean."

A sudden rage burst from his chest, like some kind of alien monster baby that had been rearing to get out.

Actually, fuck it.

"No, forget that. I don't support it." He closed the distance between them with quick strides. "I fucking hated seeing you wearing his clothes and in his apartment. I wanted to tear his hands off for touching you, and pull his tongue out of his mouth for calling you his." He shoved his fingers into her silky red locks as those bright Arctic eyes turned crystalline. "You *can't* be his. Because you're fucking *mine,*" he roared as he brought his lips down on hers in a bruising kiss. Then he lifted her up, dropped her on top of his desk, and had his way with her, in every way and six ways from Sunday.

At least, in his mind, that's how this particular scenario ended.

"Hello? Earth to Wyatt?" Curious blue eyes looked up at him as she waved a hand in front of his face. "You still in there?"

Fuck, maybe I am going insane. "Uh, yes." He blinked, calming his nerves. Where that particular fantasy—or perhaps delusion—came from, he wasn't sure, but he damned well better get ahold of himself because he had to stop thinking about his brother's girlfriend that way. "I just needed to get that out of the way."

Her delicate brows knitted together. "Get that—" Her lips parted as she sucked in a breath. "Wait a minute. You think Bastian and I ..." The expression on her face shifted quickly, from confusion to realization and finally to amusement. "You think we're having sex? Banging? Making the beast with two backs? Doing the—"

"Yes," he bit out through gritted teeth. "Aren't you?"

"Oh. My. God." Laughter burst from her mouth. "You're not serious—eww! We are not sleeping together."

"Then what were you doing at his apartment last night, wearing his clothes?"

"I was watching his new puppy, Jessica."

"Bastian has a pet?"

"Mm-hmm. I can't believe you would think—he's *Bastian*, for Christ's sake." She shuddered. "If he wasn't a Lycan, he'd be a walking STD."

Wyatt could only stare at her, dumbfounded, as a million emotions passed through him.

Mostly, it was relief. Relief that he no longer had to imagine Lizzie and Bastian having sex and that he didn't have to kill his brother.

"I can't believe ..." She shook her head. "As if Bastian would ever look twice at me."

"What?" He didn't mean to shout that word, but he'd

somehow not only lost his mind, but also control of his own mouth. "What the fuck does that mean?"

She sighed. "He's him and I'm"—she gestured to herself—"me. I mean, the last time I checked, I wasn't a blonde super-model with legs all the way down to Argentina. He's way out of my league."

"Did he say that?" Outrage burst in his chest at the idea she didn't think she was good enough for Bastian, which perhaps proved that he was indeed, going insane.

"He didn't have to. Why would someone like him want someone like me? I mean—never mind."

A glum look briefly passed across her face, one that had Wyatt itching to do something to make sure she never made it again. His wolf, too, didn't like that she has seemed so sad and urged him to make it better.

Better? He scoffed. What the hell was he supposed to do? Besides, what did it matter? He was supposed to be staying away from Lizzie. This damned fixation he had with her had to end.

Wyatt put on his most neutral expression. "Forgive me for jumping to the wrong conclusion then."

"No skin off my back." Her brows knitted together and she looked around. "Did you change anything in this office? Something smells really ... there's something about it ... I can't put my finger on." She took a deep sniff. "New carpets? Couch?"

"The only thing I changed was the chair, and I had my PC transferred here." Turning away from her, he headed toward his desk, his back to her. "You should head down to IT and check on those firewalls."

"Right. Will do."

Wyatt remained on his feet as he listened to the sound of her soft footsteps across the carpeted floor and the swoosh of the heavy wooden doors as they opened, then closed.

Fuck.

He rubbed at his jaw as he struggled to unclench it. There had to be a way to stop this ridiculous preoccupation he and his wolf had with Lizzie Martin.

She was absolutely, positively the wrong woman for him.

Though they technically grew up in the same clan, they moved in different social circles. Perhaps they'd met a time or two when they were pups, but he couldn't recall when. Then he moved to boarding school in England when he was about twelve. Even when he started working for Creed Security, he never had any business with Lone Wolf Investigations and Security, so there was no opportunity to run into her. No, Wyatt strictly stayed in the human side of the business.

But then, with their enemies growing stronger and bolder, the Alpha had no choice but to strike back, so he put together the Guardian Initiative, a team within the clan designated to ferret out and defeat the mages. When they were brought together for that first meeting, he knew he and Lizzie Martin simply would not suit.

She was childish.

Uncouth and ridiculous.

Indecorous and uncultured.

Yet, he was drawn to her that very moment. Stalked her every chance he got. Warned off any male who got too close, until well, it was him who got too close.

Ripped up fuzzy pink sweater.

Open flesh.

Blood everywhere.

Lizzie had almost died when that crazy bastard Jean-Baptiste got to her. Both he and his wolf had become unhinged when they found her all bloody and injured, and they vowed the bastard would pay. Even though Lizzie recovered, he could not control his or his wolf's need for revenge. It raged at him for failing to protect her. So, to satisfy its need for revenge, he snuck into the secret holding cell underneath Fenrir Corp where they were holding Jean-Baptiste and beat that asshole to within an inch of his life.

It had felt good, pounding his fist into the other man's face. The sound of flesh ripping and bone breaking. But it was also that moment he knew he had gone too far.

A buzz from his front coat pocket shook him out of the dark memory. Fishing his phone out, he glanced at the screen, which flashed his brother's name.

Great. The last the person he wanted to talk to. But then again, now that Wyatt knew he wasn't sleeping with Lizzie, that dreaded feeling in his chest was gone.

"Yeah?" he answered brusquely.

"Good morning to you too, sunshine." Bastian greeted. "Did you sleep well last night?"

"I did, thank you," he lied. "What is it?"

"Nothing, bro. I mean, I just wanted to check in on you. But, since I have you on the phone, I was wondering what you were doing tomorrow night? Say, around nine o'clock?"

"Tomorrow?" He strode over to his computer and opened his calendar program. "I have an early dinner meeting at six, but I should be able to wrap that up by eight."

"Great! That means you're free to come to a party."

Wyatt let out an exasperated groan. Going to one Bastian's parties was not his idea of fun. The last time he accepted his brother's invitation to go anywhere, he ended up stuck on an island in French Polynesia for a week. "Look, if you wanna grab dinner or a drink, I'll go, but I'm not going to a party with you."

"Aw, c'mon, don't be a wet blanket now. Are you still sore about Bora Bora?" He chuckled. "I promise, this one's more local. The Galveston Hotel in Soho."

"And what's this party for?"

"I'm glad you asked. Have you read *Up Close Weekly*'s Top Ten Hottest Bachelor CEOs?"

"No. Should I have?"

"Bro, I swear, sometimes I think we're not related." Bastian clucked his tongue. "You and I happen to be sharing the number seven spot this year."

"What?" The idea of appearing in some magazine made Wyatt's skin crawl. He hated press of any kind. It was vulgar.

Storming over to his desk, he opened up a browser to check the *Up Close Weekly* website. Sure enough, right on the front page was that ridiculous article. He let out an audible groan as it confirmed what Bastian told him. That tawdry gossip rag obviously took his photo and information from the Creed Security Press Release announcing his appointment as CEO a few months ago. He gritted his teeth as he read the blurb under his picture.

For the first time in our history of ranking tech's hottest CEOs, we not only have two men sharing a spot, but they're brothers, too. Sebastian "Bastian" Creed Jr., CEO of Polaris Inc. is no stranger to our list, but recently, we've discovered he has an older brother, Wyatt, who took over for their father, the senior Sebastian Creed, when he stepped down as CEO of Creed Security after it was revealed he was a Supernatural who turned into a giant, fire-breathing dragon. The two brothers were revealed to be Supernaturals themselves or "Lycans," but it's quite obvious they're both beastly and ruthless when it comes to business. Whether that extends to other activities, we'll have to use our imaginations.

"I didn't authorize this. Which bloody publicist green lit this farce?"

"Cool down, dude. And don't bite my head off, I'm just the messenger. *Up Close Weekly* does this every year. I can't believe that asshole Maxim Silver is number one. He wasn't even in the ranking last year! Anyway, you should check with your assistant, they probably sent you an invitation."

Wyatt blew out an impatient breath. "Why not bring one of your dates? Didn't I see you partying in Capri with what's-her-name? The singer?"

"This is *Up Close Weekly's* Top Ten Hottest *Bachelor* CEOs," Bastian pointed out with an exasperated huff. "I can't show up there with a date. And I guarantee if we show up together, we'll break the Internet. Think of the positive press and attention we'll generate for Lycans and our companies."

"Look, Bastian, I don't have time to go to a party with you."

"Yes you do, you just told me. Wyatt, c'mon." Bastian's tone completely changed. "Do it for me. Let's be each other's plus-ones. It's been so long since we hung out. I swear, if you hate it, we can leave and go anywhere else. Please?"

Wyatt massaged his temple. "Fine."

"Great! I'll meet you there at nine. See you!"

As he put his phone away, Wyatt mentally shook his head. He always did find it hard to say no to his brother.

That, and Bastian's powers of persuasion were unmatched. He could sell wood to a forest, and then buy it back at half the price.

Huffing, he leaned back in his chair. One party couldn't hurt. Besides, Bastian would be there. As the lingering scent of champagne and strawberries tickled his nose, he thought that at this point, if Bastian invited him to go anywhere in the world, he'd accept.

Maybe they could go someplace far away enough from Lizzie Martin—like Antarctica—so he could finally get her out of his mind.

Chapter Four

Lizzie stared up the entrance of The Galveston Hotel as she alighted from her rideshare car. Her stomach did a little flip at the thought that this could be the night Maxim Silver would finally notice her.

She smoothed her hands down her little black dress that came to her knees, which she had paired with a cute white jacket, plus high heels that added more height to her petite frame. A couple of people walked ahead of her, all of them dressed to the nines. The bouncer by the door checked their phones and IDs, which indicated the place had likely been closed down for the party. Scrolling through her phone, she found the invite Bastian had sent her, telling her to be here by nine. *Only five minutes late.* Where was he?

A limo pulled up behind her, and she stepped aside as the driver came around to the passenger side. To her surprise, a family figure stepped out.

"Wyatt?" The name flew out of her lips before she could stop herself.

His head immediately snapped toward her, hazel eyes widening. "Lizzie? What are you doing here?"

Once again, Lizzie found herself unable to tear her gaze away from him. He was wearing his usual dark suit, and his hair was impeccably styled back, though he must have forgotten to shave as a five-o'clock shadow marked his usually clean jaw. Clearly, the rugged look worked for him. And why did she never notice those flecks of green in his eyes?

Yesterday's encounter with him had left her shaken, and why, she didn't know.

No one told her that he was now the new CEO of Creed Security. He was the last person she expected to see that morning and it occurred to her that they had never been alone together in a room before. It suddenly made sense why the office was different and why the familiar lingering scent was all over the place.

Leather. Vanilla. Burnt Paper. Sweet cherries.

It wasn't until she was in the elevator when it hit her—he was the one that carried and comforted her after Jean-Baptiste attacked her and brought her back to HQ so she could receive medical attention. She would never forget that scent or his warm skin or his strong arms around her.

Why had he never said anything?

"Lizzie?"

"Huh? Oh, right. Um, Bastian asked me to come."

"Bastian?" His voice had that strange, tense edge again. "As his date?"

"As his plus-one." She emphasized that last word. "And you?"

"Aside from the fact that I'm also in this bloody magazine, Bastian also asked me to be his plus-one."

"But that doesn't make any sense." But then again, they were talking about *Bastian*.

"I—" His lips pursed as a buzzing sound came from his coat pocket. Taking it out, he glanced at the screen. "Speak of the devil. Bastian, where the—" A line appeared between his furrowed eyebrows. "Yeah, she's here." Lifting the phone away from his ear, he tapped on the video camera icon.

Bastian's grinning face appeared on the screen. "Hey, Lizzie, what's up? Nice outfit, by the way."

"Bastian, where the hell are you?"

"Uh, yeah about that." He smiled sheepishly, then moved his camera to show the interior of what appeared to be a luxury private jet. "I'm headed to Croatia."

"Croatia?" Wyatt roared.

"Yeah. A deal I'm working on is about to go tits-up. Gotta go over there and handle it personally."

"What are we supposed to do here, then?" Wyatt asked.

"Yeah, you told me to meet you here," Lizzie added.

"Uh, it's a party. Go and have fun? I mean, you're both already there, just go together."

"As dates?" Lizzie said, panicked.

"As plus-ones," Bastian said cheekily. "Oops! Captain says I gotta hang up or we'll lose our takeoff slot. Bye, guys, have fun!"

"Bastian, wait—" The screen turned black, and Wyatt muttered something under his breath before angrily shoving his phone back into his coat pocket. "Ass."

"I can't believe he just left like that," Lizzie said.

"He's my brother, I can believe it," he replied in a tight voice.

"This is a *disaster*," she cried. Maxim Silver could be

waiting inside right now. Bastian was her excuse to bump into him, but now she would have to go in by herself like some dork. Or worse, Maxim would think she was a weirdo stalker. "What are we going to do?"

"I don't know about you, but I'm going home," Wyatt grumbled, then signaled to his driver. "You can go to the party if you want."

Lizzie's stomach dropped. *Stupid Bastian.* And to think she got all dressed up to come here too. *Fine then, I'm going home too. Eames, call a car please.*

Of course ... Drivers are currently busy now. The nearest car is twenty minutes away. Would you like to wait?

"Oh God, no." Stand out here for twenty minutes by herself? Sounds like an even bigger disaster than showing up alone. "I'll take the subway. Where's the nearest one?"

It's ten blocks away.

She glanced down at her shoes. "Not in these heels." Sighing, she walked in the direction of the hotel entrance and flashed her invitation at the bouncer who let her inside.

Maybe I can hide out in the bathroom for the next twenty minutes. She could still save this disaster of an evening by going home, curling up under the covers, and watching some of her favorite comfort shows. There was no way this could get any worse.

But she shouldn't have spoken so soon, because coming out of the hallway that led to the bathrooms was the man of the hour himself, Maxim Silver. He was so preoccupied with scrolling on his phone that he didn't see Lizzie and collided right into her.

She let out a squeak as she teetered back. "Whoa!" Thankfully, Maxim had reached out and grabbed her arm, preventing her from falling flat on her ass. However, he pulled on her a little too strongly, and she ended up planting her hands on his firm, muscled chest. "I ... uh ..." She staggered back, a breath catching in her throat.

"You okay?" he asked, his voice low and thick like honey.

"I ... uh ... yeah, sorry about that." A giggle burst out of her mouth. "I'm so clumsy."

"Have we met?" His gaze narrowed at her. "You look familiar."

Lizzie died just a little bit inside but managed to speak. "Yes. I work at Lone Wolf Investigations and Security."

His brows wrinkled as though he were in deep thought. "Oh yeah. I remember. Leila, right?"

"Lizzie," she corrected.

"Lizzie. So, you're working here tonight too?"

His blue eyes were so mesmerizing, she couldn't speak and instead made a sound that sounded like, "Um, sure."

"Great." He brushed his hands over his dress shirt, which had the top two buttons undone to show a good amount of tanned skin. "Would you mind getting me a martini, then, sweetheart?"

"A ... martini?"

"Yeah. Gin martini, with a twist of lemon. And tell the bartenders to use the top shelf stuff, okay?"

Lizzie paused, then it began to sink in. He thought she was a server. Glumly, she glanced down at her white and black outfit. *That probably didn't help.* "Mr. Silver, I'm not—"

"There you are." An arm slipped around her waist. "I thought I'd lost you."

That familiar scent of leather, burnt paper, vanilla, and cherries tickled her nostrils, and her she-wolf yipped in happiness. "W-Wyatt?" She was suddenly very aware of the weight of his hand as it rested at her waist.

"You're Wyatt Creed, CEO of Creed Security." Maxim sized him up. "It's nice to meet you. Maxim Silver."

Wyatt took the hand he offered. "Nice to meet you too. You weren't trying to steal my Lizzie away, were you?"

The strangest tingle started low in her stomach at the words *my Lizzie*. She tried to open her mouth, but found that she couldn't, not when his fingers pressed against her hip.

"Your Lizzie?"

"Mm-hmm." He pulled her even closer. "She's a catch, you know. Beautiful and smart. I mean, she's the only person we trust to set up our firewalls and security systems in the building. And as you know, Creed only works with the best." The emphasis on the last two words were unmistakable. "Is Lone Wolf considering you for a client?"

"They're considering *me*?" Maxim couldn't hide the disdain in his voice.

"Lone Wolf is very selective," Wyatt added. "Especially with who works with Lizzie. She's the future of tech. She's got special talents you can only dream of. You could say she's *magic* with computers."

"I see." Maxim's nostrils flared. "Well, as I said, it was nice to meet you, Wyatt. Maybe we'll bump into each other again tonight. If you'll excuse me, a couple of photographers asked me to pose in front of the display." He pointed to the humungous mockup of the magazine cover with his face occupying the entire height of one wall.

Wyatt flashed him a smile that didn't quite reach his eyes. "Well then, we shan't keep you a minute longer."

He nodded at them, then strode away toward the awaiting photographers.

Once he was out of earshot, Wyatt sucked on his teeth. "No wonder Bastian was sore about him ranking number one."

Lizzie blinked. "Why ... why did you do that? And say those things to him?"

He loosened his grip on her, then smoothed a hand down the front of his coat. "I heard everything. What he said about you getting him a martini. Didn't sound like the first time he thought you were some lowly peon. I merely wanted to correct him."

Actually, Lizzie meant the *other* things he said. Like that part when he called her *my Lizzie*. "Um, thanks. Hey, I thought you were going home."

"I was." His jaw clenched. "I just wanted to make sure you had a ride."

"Oh. I can always call a car."

"Right."

An awkward silence stretched between them. "So," she began. "I guess you're headed out then?"

"Why don't we stay?"

Lizzie wasn't sure she heard him correctly. "Excuse me?"

"We should stay." He cocked his head toward the lobby, where the party was taking place. "I wasn't crazy about coming here, but Bastian convinced me I should do it to generate positive publicity for Lycans."

"He did?"

"Yeah." He frowned. "And we could use some goodwill these days."

Thinking back to that asshat Larry Eastman, she couldn't

disagree. "True. All right, I guess it won't hurt." Besides, all she had to do was stand around and eat canapés and drink champagne right. She wasn't exactly the social type. *Ugh.*

"Why are you frowning? Did what Silver say still bother you?"

"No, it's not that." She bit her lip. "I just ... this really isn't my scene. Parties and events, I mean. I go to them maybe once a year, at the annual New York Clan Christmas party. But that's different, because it's always the same people. I don't know the first thing about socializing."

"It's not that hard. You do some small talk, have a few drinks, laugh at people's jokes."

"Not that hard for you, maybe. You've probably been to hundreds of these parties. But what if I say the wrong thing or commit some faux pas?"

"Who cares what they think?" He shrugged. "And if you do something wrong, it's not like it'll follow you around forever. People have surprisingly short memories. Besides, you don't have to worry, I'll be here beside you the entire evening. So, what do you say? Be my plus-one?"

Lizzie stared at the hand he held out to her, her gaze moving up to the rest of him until they landed on his handsome face with that arrogant frown and those hypnotic, green-flecked light eyes. *Now I know how Adam felt in the Garden of Eden.* Tempted by the devil himself.

When she took his hand, the most curious *zing* went up her arm. "Lead the way, then."

Partying and schmoozing didn't seem as bad as it sounded in Lizzie's head. Or maybe it was because Wyatt was so good at it that she hardly had to do anything. Wyatt knew exactly what to say and when to say it, even though he had never met any of these people. He exuded a confidence that attracted people to his side and they listened when he spoke or gave his opinion about something.

"Mr. Creed, I didn't think I'd see you here." An older blonde woman snuck up from behind the moment Wyatt and Lizzie were alone, like a snake stalking prey. "Your brother attended last year, though."

"How could I miss it," he said smoothly. "You're Ellen MacDonald, Editor-in-Chief for the Manhattan Post Reader."

Lizzie recognized the name of the notorious newspaper, though calling it "news" was a stretch. They liked to use incendiary headlines as clickbait, often with a fearmongering slant, to drive traffic to their website. Most recently, the Supernaturals had been their target, and they'd been as kind to the Lycans as Larry Eastman.

She looked taken aback. "You know who I am?"

"I do my homework," he replied smoothly. "After all, you're one of the most powerful women in the New York media."

"The editor of a certain fashion magazine might beg to differ," she chuckled. "But you flatter me, Mr. Creed."

"Please, it's Wyatt."

"And you must call me Ellen," she said, placing a hand on his arm.

Lizzie gritted her teeth at the bold touch, while her wolf made its displeasure known with a soft growl.

Ellen tsked. "Whoever was in charge of fact-checking *Up Close Weekly* should be fired. I thought tonight was honoring the hottest bachelor CEOs." Her eyes darted toward Lizzie.

"I'm just his plus-one," Lizzie quickly said.

"Oh, really?" The corner of her lips curled up. "Well then—"

"Ellen, there you are. I was looking all over for you." Maxim Silver sidled up to the editor and offered her a glass of champagne. "I see your hand is empty. This should fix that."

"Handsome and considerate," Ellen exclaimed as she took the glass from him. "No wonder you're at the top spot this year. By the way, have you met Wyatt Creed?"

Maxim gave Wyatt a cool nod. "Yes, earlier this evening."

"Oh, Wyatt was about to introduce me to his lovely plus-one for the evening," Ellen said.

"My *girlfriend*, actually," Wyatt corrected.

Goose pimples prickled over her skin at the words, and her heart jumped when his hand slid around her waist once more. And as if that wasn't enough, he leaned in close to her ear and took a deep sniff. His nose never made contact with her skin, but from where Ellen and Maxim were standing, it might have looked that way.

Ellen arched an eyebrow. "And does this girlfriend have a name?"

"Lizzie Martin," Wyatt said. "You may have heard of her grandfather. Former Governor of New York, Jacob Martin."

Lizzie would have stumbled back were it not for his grip on her. Grandpa Jacob had retired from politics after his failed bid for the presidential nomination of his party a few years ago; she didn't even know Wyatt would remember him.

"Interesting," Ellen said. "*Up Close Weekly* should definitely fire their fact-checkers then."

"Perhaps you should fire yours," Wyatt said smoothly. "After that rubbish your paper's been printing about Supernaturals."

It was as if all the air had been sucked out of the entire vicinity and everything froze. A brief flash of outrage crossed Ellen's face and Maxim's blue eyes looked ready to fall out of their sockets.

Lizzie couldn't believe he'd said that. Yet, Wyatt's demeanor remained cool and unperturbed as if he'd had every right to say those words and to a powerful person to boot. And why the heck it caused a weird stirring in Lizzie's belly, she wasn't sure, but she continued to stare at him, agog.

Puzzle.

Mystery.

Conundrum.

And definitely, *what the fuck, man.*

Ellen cleared her throat delicately. "Well then, maybe you should help us correct our misconceptions. Would you be willing to sit down for an interview?"

"Have your assistant call mine to schedule a day."

"I look forward to it. Maybe I'll even do the interview myself." She eyed him like a piece of steak, which made Lizzie's inner wolf curl its lips. "We can do it one-on-one."

"Maybe you could feature my company too, Ellen?" Maxim interjected. "It's been a while since you did an article about us."

"Sure, Maxim." She patted his cheek. "Maybe in the next couple of weeks, all right? You've been on the cover of three magazines this month. Don't want you getting too over-exposed."

"Of course." He nodded to her in deference. "So, Lizzie," he began. "How is the former governor these days?"

"He's well, thanks," she replied. "Lives upstate, does a lot of fishing. We see him every major holiday, and sometimes he comes down just for a visit."

"Maybe you'll get to meet him for Thanksgiving," Maxim joked to Wyatt.

"I've met the former governor before," Wyatt snapped. "Our families are old friends."

"Right." Ignoring him, Maxim turned to Lizzie. "I guess I'll be seeing you around more often then? Since I'll be working with your company closely." He flashed her a devastatingly handsome smile.

Lizzie felt a hot blush crawl up her cheeks. "I-I guess so."

"There's Harris, the editor-in-chief," Ellen nodded across the room. "Haven't had a chance to say hello since he's been so busy. I better go over now before he disappears again."

"I'll join you," Maxim said. "I look forward to seeing you again, Lizzie."

"You do that," Wyatt added, then when the two were out of earshot, he said, "Good riddance. That woman is abhorrent."

"Sounds like you couldn't wait to sit down and be alone with her." The words were out of her mouth before she could stop herself. Her wolf, though, gnashed its teeth, wanting to hunt down the other female.

"And you? Are you looking forward to working closely with Mr. Silver? Maybe you'll be crawling under his desk by tomorrow." He too, suddenly seemed taken aback by his own words. "Lizzie, I didn't mean—"

She disentangled herself from him. "Maybe I will. Why did you think I came here in the first place?"

Fury replaced the contrition on his face. "And what is

that supposed to mean? I thought you were Bastian's plus-one?"

"So that I could come here and meet Maxim outside the office," she hissed. "I told you, I don't go to places like this."

"You want to meet ..." His Adam's apple bobbed as he swallowed hard. "You actually like that douche?"

"He's not a douche," she defended. "And so what if I do like him? He's single and rich and handsome. But now, thanks to you, he thinks I have a boyfriend, so I'll never have a chance." *Oh God, oh God, oh God, I really said that out loud.* What was it about Wyatt Creed that destroyed what little brain-to-mouth filter she did have?

"You know he's only interested in you because he thinks you're with me," he bit out. "Men like him always want what they can't have, especially if it belongs to someone else."

"Belongs to—" Lizzie froze as the words sank in. "Oh. My. God." Her jaw turned slack as the wheels in her mind began to turn.

"Lizzie? Are you all right?"

"Better than ever," she squeaked as she clapped her hands together. "Oh, Wyatt, you're a genius! I could kiss you!"

"I beg your pardon?"

"I said, you're a genius!" She gripped his arms. "In particular, what you said about men." It made sense to her now, what she had to do to catch Maxim Silver's attention. "Wyatt, you have to keep pretending to be my boyfriend."

"I—*what?*"

"We need to pretend we're together."

"Why?"

"You said it yourself." *Ugh, was he dense or something?* "I was never on his radar because I didn't belong to anyone else. But if we pretend to be boyfriend–girlfriend, then he won't be able to resist me."

A muscle in Wyatt's jaw pulsed. "That's not what I meant when I said that."

"But it makes sense." She dragged him outside toward the lobby, away from the din of the party. "As long as I'm unavailable, he'll keep chasing me." So, she *wasn't* imagining that flirty smile he flashed her before he left. *Did he really mean what he said about looking forward to seeing me?* "So? What do you say?"

"No." His jaw tensed even more. "Absolutely not. Never."

The words stung her pride like arrows hitting their mark. *He didn't have to sound like he'd rather be getting his teeth pulled than pretend to be my boyfriend.* "All right then."

"We can't—all right? What do you mean, *all right?*"

"I mean, if you don't want to be my fake boyfriend, I won't twist your arm," she said with a shrug. "Hmmm, but that would mean I would have to ask someone else. Too bad Bastian is in Croatia."

"My brother?" The words exploded from his mouth like a gunshot. "You can't be fucking serious."

"You're right." She tapped a finger on her chin. "That would be gross, since Maxim thinks we're already dating. If only I could order a fake boyfriend like I could a car—oh!" She slapped her forehead. "Of course I can." Grabbing her phone from her purse, she unlocked the screen. "Eames, download the top five dating apps onto my phone."

Right away, Lizzie.

"Bloody hell." Wyatt snatched the phone from her hand.

"Stop! Stop downloading," he shouted at the phone as he shook it violently.

Lizzie rolled her eyes. "That's not how it works." With a sigh, she took the phone back. "Look, if you won't be my fake boyfriend so I can get a real boyfriend, then I have to find someone else to help me. Unfortunately, the only men I routinely hang out with are from the office, and I'm related to most of them. Of course, there is that new guy—"

"Damn it, all right! I'll do it," he growled.

"You will? But you just said you didn't—"

"It makes ... more sense," he said through gritted teeth. "He already thinks we're dating. And this way, you don't have trawl those ridiculous app for random men. There're some truly creepy men out there."

"I'm a Lycan, Wyatt. I'm pretty sure I could handle myself if anything were to happen." She grinned at him. "But you'll really do it?"

His nostrils flared. "Yes."

"Yay!" She couldn't help but squeal in excitement. "How can I ever thank you?"

He threw a dark look over at the magazine mockup where Maxim's handsome face loomed over them. "You can start by leaving this damn party with me."

"W-with you?" A strange heat built up in her belly.

"If we're supposed to be dating, I can't just leave you here by yourself."

Oh, he meant leave at the same time. Not *together*. "Oh sure. Let me call a car then."

He shook his head. "If I'm going to be your fake boyfriend, then I should take you home, shouldn't I?"

She almost said, *my home or yours*, but managed to stop

herself. "Um, yeah sure."

"C'mon." His hand rested on the small of her back. "Let's go."

The ride to her apartment in Wyatt's limo was relatively silent. She sat on the other end of the seat, glancing back at him once in a while as he scrolled through his phone, answering emails and messages and once in a while frowning and muttering under his breath.

When they started the Guardian Initiative, most people —including Lizzie— thought Wyatt was an arrogant, stuck-up ass. He always had this air of superiority around him, like he was better that anyone else because he went to a fancy school abroad and held an important position in his father's company. He never stayed around to socialize or get to know the other members of the team, preferring to maintain a distance between him and his subordinates.

But now that Lizzie thought about it, GI ran so much smoother under his guidance. Being one of the key leaders, he ran a tight ship. He understood that what they were doing was literally life and death, and there was no space for mistakes. Maybe she'd been wrong about him.

And another layer was added to the puzzle that was Wyatt Creed.

She snuck another glance at him, her gaze drawn to his firm lips, tracing down to his jaw and neck. A memory flashed in her mind, of pressing her nose to that spot and breathing in his scent. The pulse there jumped, then Wyatt's head swung around, and their gazes met. Those light eyes almost glowed in the dim light of the limo, and once again, warmth curled in her lower belly. Her wolf let out a slow yowl.

Lizzie broke the contact immediately. "That's me up ahead, corner building, Mr. Morrison," she said as the driver turned into her street. "So, um, thanks for the ride. I should get going."

He put his phone down. "We should probably figure out how we're going to do this."

"Do this?"

"This fake dating thing."

"Oh." She thought for a moment. "I mean, maybe there won't be anything for you to do at all."

"And how do your figure that?"

"Maxim only has to *think* we're dating," she pointed out. "And now it sounds like he'll be working closely with me at Lone Wolf. I can make my move then." She waggled an eyebrow at him at an attempt at humor, but her effort fell flat as he did not react. *Everybody's a critic.* "Anyway, don't worry about it. We'll cross that bridge when we get there. So, goodnight!"

Before he could say anything, she unlatched the door handle and climbed out, quickly making her way into her building. As she took the steps two at a time, she reminded herself of her goal—to stop living life on the sidelines and take what she wanted. And she wanted Maxim Silver.

Once she reached the inside of her apartment, she closed her eyes, trying to picture his tall, dark and handsome frame and those blue eyes. However, try as she might, a different person altogether appeared in her mind's eye—someone with a serious, arrogant expression on his face and hazel eyes.

She swallowed hard. Sometimes what you wanted and what you could have were two different things.

Chapter Five

Lizzie wasn't sure when she'd have a chance to see Maxim Silver again, but she sure didn't think it would be the very next day.

Thanks to her powers, she could automate many of her daily tasks and assignments which meant she had a lot of time on her hands during the day, and she did her best to use it wisely.

And by wisely, she meant creating complete and utter chaos.

"Acme Mortuary," she answered cheerfully when her phone rang with a special ringtone she programmed. "You whack 'em, we slab 'em!"

She could hardly contain the giggle bubbling in her throat at the confused-sounding man on the other end. *That'll teach you to scam little old ladies.*

Using her powers, Lizzie convinced various phone operators' computers to reroute suspicious spam calls to her phone. Once the computers sent the callers to her, her phone would ring with a specific ringtone, and Lizzie answered just to waste their time, thus, preventing them from siphoning money from sweet old grandmas and grandpas.

Lizzie went through her usual routine, keeping the scam caller on the line, frustrating them with her ditzy, innocent act. Once in a while, if a particular caller turned nasty, she traced their call and sent them a virus to shut down their computers and servers.

"Why, sir, that language is uncalled for," she exclaimed as her latest victim screamed obscenities at her. The sound of her office door opening made her swivel her chair around. "I —Maxim?" She nearly dropped the phone when she saw him standing there. "What are you doing here?" Discreetly, she hung up on the scammer and put her phone away.

"I knocked a few times, but you didn't answer," he said. "I hope you don't mind I just opened the door."

"Oh. No. Yeah, sorry about that." Hopefully he didn't overhear her phone conversation. "Um, can I ... help you with anything?"

"Yeah, I was in the neighborhood, and I thought I'd drop by."

Standing up from her chair, she circled around her desk and strode over to him. "Isn't your office all the way downtown, by Wall Street?"

The grin he flashed her was different this time. It still oozed charm, but there was a hint of boyish sheepishness, like he'd been caught with his hand in the candy jar. "You got me," he said. "I wasn't just in the neighborhood."

Oh God, this was it! He was here to see *her*.

"I was hoping to speak with Killian regarding starting our contract. He's your uncle, right?"

So wasn't here for her. "Yeah." *Le sigh.*

"And your father is Quinn Martin? We've spoken too, but I didn't make the connection." He stepped inside. "Listen, I was wondering—"

"Mr. Silver? There you are." Uncle Killian's head poked through the door, which had been left slightly ajar. "Our receptionist told me you were here and wanted to speak with me." Keen violet eyes trained on Maxim. "May I suggest you wait in our lobby next time? It's much more comfortable there." His tone was extra polite, but it was clearly not a suggestion.

"Of course. I just wanted to say hi to Lizzie."

"Lizzie?" Now, Uncle Killian's gaze riveted to her as he pushed the door open and began to stalk closer to them. "Have you two been introduced?"

"Yes, I didn't get a chance to say goodbye to her at the party last night."

"A party?" A dark eyebrow arched up. "What were you doing at a party with Maxim?"

Oh crap. Uncle Killian might think she was a crazy stalker, going to that party just so she could bump into Maxim. *Double crap.* That was exactly what she did, which meant she *was* a crazy stalker. "I, uh ..."

"She wasn't with me, I'm afraid, but rather, with her boyfriend, W—"

"Mr. Silver is really interested in becoming our client," she interjected, stepping between the two men. *Triple crap.* Why the heck did she come up with that fake dating idea without thinking it through? No one here would believe she and Wyatt were together. And if they thought they were, she was pretty sure her overprotective father and brother would not like that bit of news. "See, Uncle K, Mr. Silver here—"

"Maxim."

"Right. Maxim would really like to hire Lone Wolf."

"And I was hoping Lizzie would work on my account," Maxim added.

"You do?" She coughed. "Er, I mean, yes, he does."

Uncle Killian crossed his arms over his chest. "I'm afraid that's not possible, Mr. Silver. Lizzie works on very special assignments and in-house only. Due to the sensitive nature of her work and to prevent conflicts of interest." He sent her a meaningful look. "Isn't that right, Lizzie?"

"Surely we can start making exceptions?" she asked, her tone hopeful.

Uncle Killian's face remained impassive. "Mr. Silver, in our initial discussion, you said you were looking to hire us as private bodyguards for events and possibly when you travel outside New York. Lizzie works purely in the IT and Cyber-security department. I'm sure being a FinTech company, you've got that part of your business covered."

"True, but because I deal with such sensitive information, I could always use an extra layer of security," he replied smoothly. "If you have time, I'd love to talk more about it. Maybe Lizzie could join us?"

"Of course, I'm always ready to talk, but Lizzie is busy at the moment."

"I am?"

"You are." The tone of his voice was unmistakable. This was an order from her boss, not her uncle.

"Right. I have to ... check on our servers."

Uncle Killian gestured to the door. "Shall we head to my office, Mr. Silver? I'll have my assistant bring us some coffee."

"Of course, Killian."

Lizzie walked with them toward the door of her office. "If you need me, just call. I'm sure I can squeeze you into my busy schedule."

Maxim beamed at her as they crossed the threshold. "Have a good day, Lizzie. Say hi to Wyatt for me."

"Wyatt?" Uncle Killian's eyebrows practically shot up to his hairline.

"Er, sure. Okay, gotta go now. Have a productive meeting." She shut the door quickly, then blew out a breath.

Oh God, please don't say anything about Wyatt to Uncle Killian, she begged silently as if Maxim could hear her pleas. Uncle Killian wouldn't understand. Hell, what was she supposed to say? *I'm not* really *dating the big boss, Uncle K. You see, I have the hots for your potential client, and I'm fake dating Wyatt so Maxim will notice me.*

It sounded so ridiculous, and on top of that, her uncle and father refused to have her work outside the office or for non-Lycan or magical clients. While she understood that Uncle Killian was only trying to protect her by keeping her powers a secret, the cat was already out of the bag.

Lone Wolf Investigations and Security was a small, tight-knit operation and only had about a dozen employees. It had started when her uncles and father had pledged to the New York Clan after being Lone Wolves—Lycans without any clan—their entire lives. Before they came to New York, the three of them, along with their sister, Aunt Meredith, had been adopted by a master thief named Archie Leacham, and he taught them everything he knew, from picking locks to hacking to social engineering. Over the years, they managed to pull off some truly spectacular heists as a team. Of course, that had changed when Aunt Meredith pledged to New York and they joined the fight to save the mages the first time over thirty years ago.

Sebastian Creed Senior had been so impressed with their work and skills that he offered them a chance to turn legit by starting a smaller offshoot of his security company. Lone Wolf Security, as it had been known back then, did work for Creed where they could use their skills as Lycans, without blowing their secret. Over the years, Lone Wolf had grown, expanding into cybersecurity, global investigations, analytics, due diligence, and security risk management. Like Lizzie, most of her cousins had joined Lone Wolf. Arch Jones was Uncle Killian's son, served as his right-hand man, and would likely take over when his father retired. Lizzie's younger brother Jacob and her cousin Cliff were agents, often working together in their overseas missions.

Though they had expanded and now had about a dozen employees, they still had to keep their natures as Lycans and hybrids a secret and so only accepted jobs vetted by Creed or the Alpha. However, since the revelation of their existence, Arch had convinced the original three Lone Wolves to at least consider opening up their client list. Uncle Killian, her father, and Uncle Connor had been resistant at first, but they also understood that now that their secret was out, their world had forever changed. Trying to go back to the way things had been would be as futile as trying to put toothpaste back in the tube.

Someone was going to find out about her powers sooner or later. Why not use it for good? Lone Wolf Investigations and Security helped people all over the world all the time. Though she loved her work, the one thing she always wished was that she could make more of a difference in the world.

Figuring she couldn't really do much at this point until hopefully Maxim could convince Uncle Killian to let her work with him, Lizzie got back to her desk, sat down and went about her morning, completing her tasks and taking on a few more calls.

"Acme Psychic Network, don't leave a message at the tone, we already know what you want."

"Lizzie?"

She spun around, and this time, she nearly fell out of her chair. Her nerve endings lit up at the sight of Wyatt Creed standing over her desk, dressed in his usual dark suit and tie, jaw clean-shaven, and light hazel eyes boring right into her. "Wyatt?"

"Should I be worried you're making prank calls during company time?"

"Er, it's for research purposes." she said. "Hi. So, what are you doing here?"

"I was in the neighborhood."

"Wow, everyone's in the neighborhood today."

"What do you mean?"

"Well, it's just that—Maxim!" She quickly shot to her feet.

"Maxim?" Wyatt's shoulders tensed when she nodded her head toward the door. "What's he doing here?"

"This is purely business." He grinned at Lizzie as he walked into her office, stopping right beside Wyatt. "And I'm happy to let you know, your Uncle Killian and I have come to an agreement."

"You've signed on as a new client?"

"On a trial basis for six months at least," he informed her. "And initially, Lone Wolf will be providing physical security for me." He leaned in her direction. "We can renegotiate later about the other things."

"What other things?" Wyatt thundered.

Slowly, Maxim straightened his shoulders and turned to Wyatt. "About Lizzie working with my company. By the way, Killian and I had the most curious conversation."

"Is that so?" Wyatt stretched to full height, which was at least half a foot taller than Maxim. "What about?"

"From what I gathered, it seems he doesn't know about you and Lizzie." He smiled smugly. "And I know why."

Fuckity fuck, fuck, he knows about the fake dating. Lizzie gripped the side of her desk. "Maxim, I can explain."

"No need." He waved her off, his gaze never leaving Wyatt's. "You own Lone Wolf. At least, Creed Security does."

Wyatt didn't show an ounce of emotion. "You've been doing your homework."

"Dating an employee," Maxim tsked. "It's not a good look."

"We have liberal fraternization rules, and Lizzie is not my direct subordinate. Besides, I've only been CEO for a few months. But truth be told, I've wanted Lizzie for a while now."

"You do?" Air sucked out of Lizzie's lungs. *He's just making up a cover story,* she reminded herself, but that did not stop her stomach from doing a flip. "Er, I mean, you did?"

"I've been abroad for years, working with Creed's international arm. But then my father asked me to come back to do a special project, and I couldn't say no. Lizzie was on that project too."

"And you couldn't make a move on her then?" Maxim concluded.

"No. That and I told you, our families have known each other for years, so it's a complicated dynamic."

Maxim folded his hands behind him. "So, it's more personal than business."

"Yes."

"We've been waiting for the right time to tell them." *Lizzie, you're a genius!*

"To let them know our relationship is solid," Wyatt added.

"Or in case anything happens and things become awkward."

"Anything happens?" Wyatt's head snapped toward her.

"Yeah," she chuckled. "I mean, we're not *that* serious."

"*Yet.*" He turned back to Maxim. "But we are exclusive."

"Until we aren't!" Lizzie burst out.

"I see." Maxim gave a dramatic pause. "I understand. I know what it's like, having everyone scrutinize every move you make, especially those closest to you. And don't worry, I didn't say a word to Killian about you two. Actually, I have a great idea."

"What is it?" Lizzie asked.

"I'm hosting a housewarming party this weekend at my new place down in Miami Beach. I'd love for you both to come. It's totally private, and my guests are always discreet. They won't gossip about you, and they likely won't know who you are, but you might know some of them." He winked at her. "You can unwind and not have to worry about sneaking around."

Wyatt opened his mouth, but before he could say anything, Lizzie interrupted him. "Sounds great, we're in."

"What?" Wyatt's hazel eyes widened. "Just—"

"Excellent. You can ride in my jet, Lizzie, in case you want to throw off any suspicions."

"We'll take my jet, thank you very much," Wyatt said sourly.

"The welcome dinner for all guests is at seven on Saturday, but feel free to arrive anytime during the day. My secretary will send yours the other details. Lizzie, it was nice seeing you again. Don't forget to bring a swimsuit." Maxim nodded politely at Wyatt before he marched out.

Wyatt threw his hands in the air. "Why in the world would you say yes to going to Florida with him?"

"I said yes to going to Florida with you," she corrected. "Besides, I couldn't say no. Then he'll really think our relationship is fake."

"It is fake."

"Yet you sold it so well too. Good thinking, telling him you've been interested in me for months." She punched him playfully on the arm. "You're great at this lying thing."

"And what made you think I wouldn't be?"

"Well ..." She tapped a finger on her chin. "You've always been a by the book, follow all the rules, uptight kind of guy."

"Uptight?"

"You never heard what people say about you?"

"I do, but I just don't give a fuck."

Truth be told, that was probably what she liked most about him.

Wait a minute.

Like?

No, she couldn't like anything about him. She liked *Maxim*. "Anyway, if you don't want to go down to Florida, I could always go by myself."

Wyatt muttered something under his breath. "That's not going to work. He thinks we're a couple, so I'll have to come with you."

"Oh, right." Puffing out a breath, she sat back down on her chair. "This whole fake dating thing is ridiculous. Maybe we should break up already."

"*No.*"

"No? But I already have his attention, plus, he'll be working with Lone Wolf regularly so I get to see him. That'll give us a chance to get to know each other. I don't really need a fake boyfriend at this point." She drummed her fingers on the table surface. "In fact, you're only hindering me now. He probably won't make a move while you're around."

"You don't have him on the hook yet." Wyatt turned all cool again, then sat down on the chair opposite to her. "Are you really sure he's interested in you? What if we 'break up,' and when he sees you're available again, he'll decide you're no fun to chase? Do you want to take the chance now, after all the effort you've put in? It's a real gamble this early in the game, and you don't even know what his cards are."

"Crap, you're right." Her teeth chomped on her lower lip. "I wish I knew more about men. Why can't you guys be more like computers? At least then, I'd be able to get into your heads and find out what you want."

"Unfortunately, Lizzie, men aren't that complicated, and we only want one thing."

"One thing? What is it?" She stared up at him, waiting

for him to answer. He remained silent, but tilted his head to the side and waited. "*Oh.*"

Sex.

He was talking about sex.

A furious blush crept up her neck, blooming all the way up to her cheeks.

His gaze narrowed at her. "Are you all right?"

"Huh? Uh, yeah." She took a deep breath. "So, uh, okay, no breaking up then."

"And now we have to go to Miami this weekend." From the tone of his voice, he might as well have said, *I need a root canal this weekend.*

"Oh yeah. Sorry about that. I know you're busy and all—"

"It's all right, believe it or not, I do try to keep my weekends free." He stood up. "We'll leave Saturday at three p.m. I'll come to yours and pick you up."

"Sounds like a plan."

"I'll see you then." With a curt nod, he left.

"Oh God." Lizzie crossed her arms on top of her desk and buried her face in her arms. When did this all become so complicated? All she wanted was to experience life and to no longer be left behind. To be a normal girl, with a normal life and a normal boyfriend. Was that too much to ask?

Her heart plummeted to the floor as another realization hit her: Maxim was probably an experienced lover and would expect anyone he took to bed to be the same.

It wasn't like she was raised in a convent and didn't know what sex was or never even had an orgasm. She'd kissed a boy before, during one of their family vacations on a cruise when she was fifteen and had to attend those silly group activities where other teenagers like her were forced to interact.

The experience was enjoyable enough, but after that, when she started school, all her male classmates were over eighteen, and none of them would even look at her, and those that did, well, she made sure they got what they deserved somehow.

And after she left that semester, there really wasn't time for boys. Her world behind the screen was safe and comfortable. It wasn't like she had any other female friends to talk to about it. Her closest pals growing up were her cousins Charley and Olivia, and they were off doing their own thing. Plus, when she did get curious about sex, she turned to the one place she did know—the Internet. Whenever she was tense or bored, all she had to do was turn to her collection of battery operated boyfriends.

But, she had no experience whatsoever in the real thing. From what's she'd watched and read about, there was more to sex than just getting off with a vibrating toy. How did one initiate sex anyway? Where did the hands go when you weren't doing anything? Didn't it chafe?

All these things, and more, she didn't know how to get the answers, except through experience. Maxim likely had a lot of it, and she would only disappoint him when it became obvious she didn't know what she was doing.

So, to sum it all up: to get a boyfriend, she needed a boyfriend. And to have sex, she needed to have sex first.

She was trapped in Catch-22 hell.

"Damn it."

Chapter Six

Wyatt truly did like to keep his weekends free. Usually, on Saturdays, he would go to his club and play racquetball, see a museum exhibit or art show, or fly off to spend the weekend at his Vermont or California home. However, ever since he took over as CEO of Creed, he'd had to put in extra hours at the office, including weekends. There was just so much to do and not enough time to do it because they were still in transition mode. His father assured him that once everything was settled, he could have a more normal schedule.

On this particular Saturday, however, Wyatt was not getting anything done. He trudged into the empty office around ten, sat down, and stared at his computer. There were no calls to make since everyone else was out. And no matter how hard he tried, none of the emails he read or documents he perused made any sense. His brain simply refused to retain any information. The only thing that did capture his attention were the four numbers on the top right side of the computer screen, indicating the time. He drummed his fingers on the table, as if willing it to move faster.

Was this thing broken? he thought, irritated.

Anticipation grew as the clock counted down. As soon as the numbers changed to "02:30," Wyatt practically flew out of his chair, made his way out of his office, and into the waiting elevator.

"Why the hell is this thing so slow?" he muttered to no one in particular. It was Saturday, for God's sake, there was no one else using the elevators. When the car did finally reach the lobby, he rushed out the door and into his waiting car.

I'm just eager to get this whole trip over with, he reasoned with himself. It didn't have anything to do with the person he was about to see.

Why the hell did I agree to this?

This entire plan was crazy, but it was his fault for trying to white knight her in the first place the night of the party. His limo hadn't even reached the end of the block when his wolf growled at him for leaving Lizzie alone. Since the beast continued to be combative, he figured he should at least offer Lizzie a ride home. When he entered the hotel, he saw her just as she bumped into Maxim and heard their entire conversation.

Maxim Silver just looked so smarmy and smug, and Wyatt couldn't believe he mistook Lizzie for some secretary at Lone Wolf. Of course, there could have been a better way to tell him he was mistaken, but his wolf was so furious at the sight of Lizzie's hands on him that he was spurred into action. After that, he just couldn't leave her alone.

He found himself enjoying the party with her at his side.

Something about it felt right—having his hands on her, smelling that delicious scent of hers, having her pressed up to him. His wolf, too, was content and happy.

His stomach tightened as they neared Lizzie's apartment, while his wolf, sensing his tension, paced around. To his surprise, she was already standing at the curb. Morrison got out and took her overnight bag, then opened the door for her.

"Hey," she greeted as she scooted inside.

"Hi." When the subtle scent of strawberries and champagne wafted into his nostrils, his wolf let out a satisfied sigh and settled down.

She remained on the other end of the seat, faced away from him, but he could see the tension in her shoulders. "Everything okay?"

"Huh?" Her head snapped toward him. "Uh, yeah." She crossed one leg over the other, then bounced it up and down. "All fine."

A lie, but Wyatt did not pry. Regret, however, seeped into his mind. Maybe she, too, was having second thoughts. Going back to the events of the night of the party, he could say it was his fault she came up with that fake dating scheme to attract Maxim. He was the one who claimed her as his girlfriend, after all. That, too, felt so right, and the look on Maxim's face was worth it.

It was once he was alone at home—away from her intoxicating scent and presence—that logic and reason took over. Pretending to be her boyfriend was an inane and terrible idea. He did not like deception and games, and if Lizzie wanted to attract Maxim, she would have to find some other way. Seeking to remedy it, he decided to tell her face-to-face, which was why he went to Lone Wolf.

But then that asshole Maxim showed up too, and he just saw red. The idea that Lizzie and Maxim would be working together closely gnawed at him, and his wolf urged him to put a stop to it. So, he was drawn deeper into this game.

Wyatt fought the urge to glance over at Lizzie, and thankfully, they soon arrived at the tarmac and boarded the Creed Security private jet.

"Good afternoon, Mr. Creed, Miss Martin," the uniformed flight attendant greeted. "My name is Henry, and I'll be flying with you today. Welcome aboard."

"Oh wow," Lizzie's eyes were the size of saucers as she took in the interior of the private jet. "So, this is how the other half lives, huh?" She bit her lip. "I should have worn something nicer."

"You look fine," Wyatt said as he came up behind her. Today she was actually wearing a "normal" outfit, at least for her—blue jeans, white canvas shoes, and a T-shirt with 'Feminism is my second favorite F word' scrawled on the front.

"Liar," she joked. "Don't worry. I Googled 'Miami party wear' and ordered some nice sundresses for the party, along with a new bikini."

Wyatt's throat went dry at the image of Lizzie in a bikini.

"*Niiiiiccce.*" Lizzie whistled as the flight attendant motioned for her to take the seat on the left. She sat down, doing a little wiggle on the leather seat.

Wyatt settled into his usual chair, located across from her. "It's certainly comfortable."

"*Pffft.*" She rolled her eyes in that way Wyatt couldn't help but find adorable, then crossed her legs. "We're not all billionaires, you know. *Mmm,*" she moaned as she sank deeper into the chair. "Like *buttah.*"

As she relaxed, Wyatt, too, felt more at ease. He didn't like seeing her so anxious, especially when he didn't know why and thus couldn't fix it.

"You know," she continued. "I flew first class once on a family vacation to Cabo. I, uh, convinced the check-in agent's computer to give me an upgrade. Jacob was pretty pissed." She chortled. "Unfortunately, I was only sixteen, and my mom made me switch with this little old lady. Oh!" Her face brightened when Henry offered her champagne. "This could be my life if only I was inclined to use my powers for evil."

"No, thank you," Wyatt waved away the flute Henry tried to hand him. "I'm just glad those bullets didn't kill me and my parents didn't have to get ball gags sent to them."

Lizzie was mid sip, so she choked on the bubbly liquid, making her eyes water as she swallowed hard. Henry took the glass from her and offered her a napkin. "Y-you remember that?" she asked, wiping her mouth.

Wyatt mentally kicked himself. The ringing from his front pocket interrupted him. To his surprise, his mother's name popped up on the screen. "Mom? Is everything okay?"

"Wyatt," Jade Creed greeted. "I'm fine, don't worry," she said with a reassuring chuckle.

He relaxed into his chair. "Good. Did you need anything?"

"No, not at all, I just wanted to check in on you because your assistant called me about tomorrow."

"Uh, yeah, sorry for canceling lunch." The tinge of disappointment in her voice made him inwardly cringe. "I'll make it up to you. Name what day you want to do dinner next week, and I'll change whatever plans I have."

"Thank you, honey. I'll check with your father and let you know, okay?"

"Sounds great."

"Love you, Wyatt."

"Love you too, Mom." He placed the phone back in his pocket. "What's wrong?" he asked Lizzie, who was staring at him, a worried expression on her face.

"I'm so sorry." Her eyes cast downward. "For making you miss dinner with your mom."

"It's fine."

"I have a mom, too, you know, and so I know all about the guilt trips. It's their God-given right." She took a tentative sip of her champagne. "You know, your mom was really worried about you. Back in Lake Hope. When you—you know, were hurt." A slight blush tinted her cheeks.

"She's my mother, of course she was."

Placing the flute on the console next to her, she leaned forward. "Aren't you close to her? Your whole family seems pretty tight-knit."

Another wave of guilt washed over him. "It's complicated."

"How?" she asked with a tilt of her head.

"I kind of grew up away from them. Dad wanted all of us to have the chances he never had since he grew up poor. You know, to have the best and be the best. I'd always dreamed of going to school in England, like Mom did, so I applied and was accepted to boarding school when I was thirteen."

"Boarding school? Must have been lonely."

"Not at all. I had a lot of fun, and my grandmother lived in London, so I got to see her all the time."

"Neat." Lizzie sat cross-legged on the seat and planted

her chin on her palms. "I never grew up with a grandmother. What was yours like? Did she bake cookies and knit you sweaters?"

He almost wanted laugh. Fiona Hastings probably didn't even know she had a kitchen as she had servants at her beck and call. "No, she wasn't that kind of grandmother, I'm afraid. She's very proper." So proper, in fact, that she didn't care much for her Lycan side. In fact, no one, not even her English husband, knew about her secret.

You must never allow that savage side of you out, Wyatt. You must learn to control the vicious beast as I have and tame your feral nature.

Indeed, Wyatt couldn't sense his grandmother's wolf, not even a faint whiff of it.

"I can't imagine living away from my family at such a young age. At least you had a relative with you there. Did she spend much time with you?"

"As much as she could, especially during my university years and while I was working in London. I also spent a lot of holidays with her and her husband."

"No wonder I never saw you during the New York Clan Christmas parties," she said. "But why didn't your parents and siblings fly over?"

"I tried to invite them, but they didn't want to come." There was still a tinge of bitterness left in his mouth at the memory.

"Oh? Didn't your mom want to see her mother?"

"Fiona and Mom have a ... strained relationship."

"Why?"

He shrugged. "They've been that way even before I was born." Neither side would say why. Wyatt had hoped that he would have been good reason enough for mother and daughter to reconcile, but apparently not. *I won't stop you from having a relationship with her, if that's what you want,* his mother had said when he turned eighteen. *You shouldn't have to pay for my choices. But just know that she's not what she seems.* Fiona, on the other hand, refused to talk about the past, and acted like everything was just fine even though she'd only seen her daughter a handful of times in the last thirty years or so.

"She must have been so sad when you left to come back to New York."

"She was disappointed." Disappointed was perhaps a mild word. She'd been *livid*, threatening to never see him again if he moved back to the States and got involved with Lycan business.

An uneasy feeling pooled in his stomach at the memory. He had felt pulled in different directions, and for a while, he was ashamed to admit now, Fiona's hold on him had been stronger than his family's. His mother had asked him many times over the years to spend more time at home, but he always found some excuse.

But if he were truly honest with himself, perhaps it was because in London, he felt freer. No one knew who or what he was.

And there was no father to seek approval from.

It wasn't that Sebastian Creed was a bad dad. In fact, he truly loved all his children. Wyatt, as the oldest son, wanted to do him proud, pushing himself to excel in everything he did. He got the best grades, top trophies in different sports, and awards in all kinds of extra-curricular activities.

Bastian, on the other hand, did whatever the hell he

wanted, got kicked out of numerous private schools, and never finished university, but Dad still treated him like the favored son. Sebastian had been so proud of Bastian especially when he started his own tech company and becoming independent at the age of nineteen, much like he did when he joined the Marines. The older Creed had seen much of himself in his younger son, more so than his older one.

Wyatt didn't resent it and never blamed Bastian, but perhaps that's when he started drifting away. Fiona was so proud of him, getting into Eton and Cambridge, then London Business School for his MBA. His grandmother repeated how she was so proud of him, not just of all he'd accomplished on his own, but of rising above his base, Lycan nature.

"Why did you come back? Sounds like you had a pretty sweet time back there."

Wyatt shrugged. "This was life and death. The fate of the world and such. I couldn't just stand by and do nothing. You heard about what happened in the past to our parents. How could I say no?"

"True." She shuddered. "To think how close we were to the Apocalypse ..."

A dead silence hung between them, until finally, she spoke. "Wyatt?"

"Yes?"

Her teeth chomped into her lower lip. "That night ... why did you do it?"

"Do what?"

"You disobeyed the Alpha's orders by running back to the van. Then you went all berserk. I mean, you remember that part, right?"

"Excuse me, Mr. Creed, Miss Martin?" Henry interrupted. "We're about to take off. Please fasten your seatbelts."

"Thank you, Henry."

They settled into their seats, and the plane took off. Once they reached cruising altitude, the fasten seatbelt signs turned off.

Wyatt was waiting for Lizzie to ask about that night again, but to his relief, she didn't bring it up. Henry served them a light afternoon snack, which was actually a traditional afternoon tea Wyatt had grown fond of during his years in England. Lizzie had never had one and was delighted at the tiers of sandwiches, cakes, and scones with clotted cream and jam.

After they finished eating, she asked if she could poke around the plane, to which he gladly agreed. He opened his tablet to catch up on some work while she explored. When the captain announced they were about to land, she bounded back to the main cabin and sat down.

"Thanks for letting me have a look around." She buckled her seatbelt. "I had lots of fun."

"Did you find anything interesting?"

"Yeah, lots. Your plane is really nice. The navigation system was quite rude and refused to talk to me, though"—her mouth twisted as she tapped a finger on her forehead—"that's probably a good thing. The galley microwave, on the other hand, is hilarious! I nearly peed my pants when it told me a story about—"

"We're landing soon," Henry announced. "Thank you for fastening your seatbelts, and I hope you enjoyed the flight. Let me know in advance if you have any special requests for tomorrow's return."

Lizzie settled into her seat, and Wyatt stared out the window as they descended through the clouds. Once they were past the layer of white, the sparkling blue ocean lay under them. He couldn't help but wonder why he had told her so much about himself and his past. It brought back too many memories, as well as regrets. He'd never opened up that way to anyone, not even to the few friends he kept over the years or previous girlfriends. Not that he had a lot of those. There was one university girlfriend his first year, but after that, it was all casual dating and a one-night stand here and there. Over the years, he'd been choosier about his companions, and he rarely spoke to them about his family. Yet with Lizzie ...

This was just one weekend, he told himself. One night, then tomorrow they'd be back in New York, and maybe they could even put this whole fake relationship behind them.

A car had been waiting for them by the time they arrived, which then whisked them toward the city. Now, they were crossing a long bridge which connected the mainland to Point Creek Island, an exclusive neighborhood just off Miami Beach. Some people called it Billionaire Island, and it was where several well-known celebrities, politicians, and businessmen had vacation getaways. A few years ago, Wyatt had been offered a piece of property there, but he had found it too gauche. The houses were just too big and their designs too trendy for his taste.

The vehicle slowed and then pulled into a driveway, and just as Wyatt had predicted, the house was the typical modern monstrosity, all glass and steel and done up in neutral tones. Cold and impersonal with no character or history.

"Holy moly." Lizzie gasped when they alighted from the car. She took off her sunglasses to admire the sprawling structure. "Wow, it's so big."

"I've seen bigger," he scoffed. If she liked big houses, then she should see his estate in Vermont. It had been his first purchase, prime property with fifty acres of wooded area and a humungous log-style cabin.

"Welcome, Mr. Creed, Miss Martin." A man in a white linen shirt and khaki pants greeted them. "My name is Eduardo, and I'm Mr. Silver's butler." He gestured to the young woman in a maid's uniform behind him, who had glasses of juice on a tray. "Please, help yourself to some refreshments."

"Is that mango?" Lizzie picked up a glass and took a sip. "Fresh too!"

"Mr. Silver has them imported straight from the Philippines," Eduardo said proudly.

Wyatt shook his head when the maid pushed the tray in his direction. "I'm fine. Where's Mr. Silver?"

Lizzie froze at the mention of the name.

"He's been delayed, I'm afraid," Eduardo explained.

While he thought he was imagining things at first, he didn't miss the way her shoulders slackened. There was definitely something going on with Lizzie.

"But he assured me he will be here in time for dinner. A few of the guests have already arrived and are now getting settled in. If you could follow me, I'll make sure you can do the same."

Eduardo led them inside, and the decor was as Wyatt had imagined. All sleek and modern, with an open floor plan that made the place like one giant box. Still, he begrudgingly gave Maxim some props because the views of the ocean were gorgeous.

"How big is this place?" Lizzie asked as they walked across an enormous wooden deck with an infinity pool at the edge.

The butler waved his hand around him. "Sixteen thousand square feet. It has a boat dock, two pools, a cinema, gym, club room, plus twelve bedrooms, eight of them in the guesthouse." He pointed up ahead to the smaller structure perpendicular to the main house. "That's where you'll be staying. All the rooms have ocean views."

They entered the guesthouse—which was probably the size of a typical Midwest McMansion—and followed Eduardo into a hallway with several doors. He opened one of them. "Here you go."

Lizzie dashed in and gasped. The main room had a small living area with a love seat, an armchair, a coffee table, and large glass doors that led to a spacious balcony. "It's bigger than my apartment. Can I see the rest?"

"Of course, Miss Martin. If you go into the dressing area, you'll see that your bags are already there since they were rushed ahead as soon as you landed."

"Thanks." With a soft squeal, she disappeared into the door on the right.

The butler gestured to the built-in console opposite the couch, which had several bottles of liquor and wine, a coffee pod machine, and a mini fridge. "Your guest room is fully stocked, but if you need anything just pick up the phone and we'll do our best to accommodate you. We'll be serving cock-tails in an hour out on the deck, so please do come as Mr. Silver has invited a famous bartender to make drinks. I hope you enjoy your stay with us."

Once Eduardo left, Wyatt headed toward the door where Lizzie went into. "Lizzie?"

"I'm here." Even from where she stood on the other side of the room, he could sense the anxiety radiating from her as she wrung her hands.

"What's wrong?"

"The bed."

"And?"

"There's only one."

He opened his mouth, then snapped it shut. There was, indeed, only one king-sized bed.

Fuck.

Of course Maxim would have them in one room. Why would he think otherwise? "I can take the couch."

"Have you seen that thing? Have you looked at yourself in the mirror? Unless you know how to fold yourself in half, you'll never fit in it. I barely can."

There was, of course, only one solution. "Then we'll sleep on this bed."

"At the same time?"

"No, in shifts." His eyes slid heavenward. "Yes, at the same time. It's a huge bed. We can put a pillow between us and we'd still both have plenty of space."

"Isn't there any other way?"

Crossing his arms over his chest. "I could always tell Maxim you snore loudly and I need my own room."

"Why do I have to be the one who—oh." She threw her

head back and laughed. "Well, slap my ass and call me Sally, Wyatt Creed actually made a joke."

The corner of his mouth tugged up involuntarily. "Enjoy it now because I'll never do it again." He walked over to her. "If it bothers you that much, I can make up an excuse to go back to New York. Just say the word, Lizzie." Every fiber in his being said that there was no fucking way he would leave her here. But he would respect her boundaries. He would hate it, but he would not force his presence on her.

Still, the knot in his chest grew as she bit at her lip, seemingly contemplating an answer. "*Pfft.*" She waved a hand at him, the tension dissipating. "We're adults, right? It's not like I've never slept beside anyone in bed before."

"Of course." He managed to strangle the growl that threaten to rip from his throat as he imagined her naked in bed with some other man. "If you don't mind, I'm going to check in with the office."

"Okay, I'm gonna unpack and get ready for dinner. I won't take too long if you need the bathroom."

Wyatt headed out of the bedroom and grabbed his tablet, then connected to the free Wi-Fi as he sank down on the armchair. As he waited for his emails to download, he leaned back and inhaled deeply.

I shouldn't be doing this. He was supposed to be staying away from temptation, but yet, he'd be closer than ever. He'd even be sleeping right next to it.

If only there was a way to take temptation away from him instead.

Maybe there was.

Bolting upright, he said, "That's it."

He knew the solution to his problem. In fact, he didn't

have to do anything at all as he was already well on his way to getting rid of Lizzie. Because once she belonged to someone else, he would have no choice but to cease this ridiculous obsession with her.

His wolf protested with a sharp yip, but he pushed it deep inside him where he wouldn't be able to hear it. Grandma Fiona always told him that in time, he too would learn to control it so well he wouldn't even know it was there. Before coming back to the States, he couldn't even remember the last time he shifted, perhaps only during the Blood Moon. That was the only instance the wolf sides were in charge, and like other Lycans, he had a special room where he could do it safely. He often wondered how Grandma Fiona had managed to hide it from her husband all those years while he was alive.

"I'm done." Lizzie bounded into the room, wearing a blue floral-printed sundress. "I hope this is okay?" She twirled around, sending the skirt flying around her, her red curls bouncing around her pretty face.

"Uh." The linen dress was retro-style with a halter neck and sweetheart neckline, showing off a generous amount of her shoulders and cleavage. "It's—"

"Are you—noooo!" Lizzie screamed and bolted to his side, grabbing his tablet, "Stop! Disconnect!"

"What the—what's the matter with you?"

"You connected to the Wi-Fi?" She held the device away from him, which was ridiculous because he was twice her size and could easily snatch it back.

"Yeah? So what? I have a VPN. Our IT set it up, and if I recall correctly, you and your father designed the security system."

She *tsked* and snapped the laptop shut. "Never, ever connect to a network you don't know. And never over Wi-Fi." She shuddered. "I hate Wi-Fi."

"Really? I thought you spoke to machines?"

"Yeah, but I need to be touching them or a computer connected to them." Her eyes darted around. "Wi-Fi creeps me out, especially the free kind, because I can't talk to it. Just, trust me, okay?"

"Fine, I'll get data through my phone. Is that okay?"

"Better," she said. "But you really need to let me lock your shit down. I'll come by your office Monday, so show me everything—your laptop, tablets, phones, and smartwatches, okay? Come to think of it, as CEO of Creed Security, you really should have had me and Dad check everything like we did for your dad."

"Yes, ma'am."

Smirking at him, she handed him his tablet back. "There. He's all good now. I told him he was a naughty boy, automatically connecting to the network like that. I threatened to spank him next time he did it."

Something about the way she said the words, dressed so provocatively like that and—*fuck*—wearing red lipstick, made his cock twitch involuntarily.

Jesus Christ, he wasn't going to survive the weekend.

"Are you going to get ready?"

"Uh, yeah." He shot to his feet. "Give me five minutes."

Brushing past her, he headed to the bathroom. Closing the door behind him, he strode over to the sink to splash water on his face.

Just make it until tomorrow. Then he'd have to start

thinking about an exit strategy so she could be with Maxim and he'd never have to think about her again.

After some time, he managed to calm himself enough so he could unpack his things and prepare for the evening ahead. He changed out of his suit and into a more casual outfit of white pants, a dark blue shirt, and navy loafers without socks.

"Hey, did you—" Lizzie stopped, her eyes widening as he entered the living area.

"What?"

Her entire face was red. "I'm, uh, nothing. You look ... different."

"Different?" He glanced down at his outfit. "I'm still wearing my clothes."

"Yeah, but it's not your usual suit."

"You don't like it?"

"I didn't say that," she replied quickly. "It's nice. I do like it." She turned her gaze away, as if she found something interesting on the opposite wall. "Er, we should get going if we're gonna make it to cocktails."

"I suppose so." He offered his arm. "Shall we?"

"S-sure."

As they made their way outside, the only thing Wyatt could think of was that having Lizzie on his arm felt like the most natural thing in the world. When they stepped out into the deck and a soft breeze blew her scent his way and sent a lock of her hair brushing against his arm, an unfamiliar sensation grew in his chest.

"Lizzie, Wyatt, you made it." Maxim walked over to them, away from the group of guests he'd been chatting with.

That strange sensation dissipated, only to be replaced with loathing. "Silver," he murmured in response.

"Your house is amazing," Lizzie gushed.

"Thank you. I didn't do much though, you'll have to compliment my real estate agent and my interior designer." When Maxim flashed them a dazzling smile, Wyatt did not fail to notice that his white teeth looked extra bright against his tan that had definitely *not* been there a few days ago. "I'm glad you made it, especially since it sounds like Lone Wolf keeps you pretty busy."

"Thank you for the invite."

"Of course. And you look lovely, by the way."

Her body tensed when his eyes ran up and down her body. "Th-thank you."

Wyatt sidled closer to Lizzie. "Do you think we could have a drink, Silver? Your butler told us you have a world-famous bartender tonight."

"Ah, yes. Will Dareen. Flew him in from Ibiza. Come, let's get you some drinks, then I'll introduce you to the other guests." He lowered his voice and leaned in. "But please respect their privacy, and don't be offended if they don't want to take selfies with you, okay?"

It took all of Wyatt's strength not to roll his eyes. "Of course."

Maxim brought them over to the bar and introduced the world-renowned mixologist to them. Lizzie ordered some fancy cocktail that was served on a wooden plank with a glass dome. She *oohed* and *aahed* when she lifted the glass and curling smoke dissipated to reveal her drink. Wyatt, on the other hand, ordered a neat scotch whiskey, much to the disappointment of the famed bartender.

Once they got their drinks, they were introduced to Maxim's "celebrity guests." Despite the fact that he wasn't into pop or celebrity culture, Wyatt knew most of the guests were C-list at best. There was some singer who had a one-hit wonder with his band about a decade ago, a former football champion and his model wife, and an aging actor whose last blockbuster was probably twenty years ago. Most of the guests were happy to snap photos and selfies and take videos on their phone, probably to share on their social media profiles where they still had some clout. Still, he managed to mingle with them, not really listening to their stories, but rather, concentrated on watching Lizzie. She looked more at ease, relaxing against his hand where he had placed it on the small of her back.

Sometime after sunset, Eduardo appeared to inform them dinner was ready. It was an elaborate affair set up in the second-floor dining room and featured ten courses of Japanese-Peruvian fusion dishes. Lizzie and Wyatt sat closest to their host, and while she once again gushed over the dishes, she was tongue-tied whenever Maxim complimented her or made any flirty overtures, which in turn, irritated Wyatt and his wolf to no end.

"Wyatt sang praises of your skill, I hope I get to see them in action myself," Maxim said to Lizzie. "If he's anything like me, then we probably have the same requirements and tastes." He eyed her over the rim of his wine glass, then added, "When it comes to security, I mean."

Wyatt fumed. *The nerve of the man.* He was sitting right beside Lizzie, and he had the audacity to—

"*Eeep!*" Lizzie knocked her glass over, spilling the contents over the table. A uniformed server quickly came by to mop up the liquid as she shot to her feet and jumped back. Wyatt followed and pulled her aside just in time before she bumped into the poor fellow. His arm snaked around her waist and pulled her against him, her plush ass pressing right against his crotch, sending his cock springing into a full erection.

Christ.

"Sorry," he murmured, releasing her quickly. "Um, some wine spilled on me. I should clean it off." He dashed off to the guest bathroom, slamming the door behind him.

Get a hold of yourself.

She was just a woman. He could have any woman he wanted. Perhaps maybe this was the result of prolonged abstinence. When was the last time he'd been with anyone? He couldn't even remember.

With deep breaths, he managed to calm himself—and his dick—down. By the time he got out, the dining room was empty, and Eduardo informed him that everyone had moved down to the pool deck for after dinner cocktails.

"Oh good, he's back!" Maxim announced. "Come on, Wyatt, we've been waiting for you. Ashlyn's come up with a great game for us."

"Me?" he asked as he walked over to them. "Why?"

Ashlyn, who had earlier introduced herself as an "influencer" with over two million followers on social media, shoved her blinged-out phone in his face. "We're doing one of those challenges on the ClockApp!"

"What's a ClockApp?"

"It's a video sharing social media app." She clucked her tongue. "Anyway, we need you for it."

"Why me?"

"Not just you. It's a couple challenge." She waved to the other guests, who were paired up with their partners. Lizzie stood by herself at the end. "I'm gonna film each one of you, and you have to listen to what the app says and follow the directions, okay?"

"No, thank you," Wyatt grumbled. "I'm not into games."

Ashlyn pouted. "Aww, you're no fun. Maxim, why don't you pair up with Lizzie?"

He smoothed a hand down his shirt. "Sure."

Wyatt's blood pressure shot through the roof. "Fine, I'll do it," he grumbled, then trudged over to Lizzie.

"You really don't have to," she whispered. "We could just tell them we're tired and go back to the room."

Back to the room, where that one bed awaited them. That sounded like the best and worst idea at the same time. "No, it's fine. It's just a silly little game."

"Okay, everyone, get ready!" Ashlyn waved her phone in the air, then pointed it at the first couple—the singer and his young husband, who was probably twenty years his junior. "And ... go!"

The phone's creepy AI voice started issuing challenges, which the couples had to do or act out, such as "point at who leaves the laundry on the floor" and "carry your partner over your shoulder."

"Last one," Ashlyn declared as she reached Wyatt and Lizzie. "What could it be?"

The app called out, "Give us your most spicy kiss!"

"Ooh!" Ashlyn squealed as the rest of the guests cheered. "C'mon guys."

Lizzie stiffened; her face paralyzed by obvious fear.

Whether it was due to fear of being found out or having to kiss Wyatt, he wasn't sure. "All right, this game is over."

"Spoilsport!" Ashlyn stamped her feet. "It's just a kiss. You must have done it hundreds of times by now."

"Maybe he's afraid we'll think he's not a good kisser," the former football champ jeered.

"It's okay," Lizzie urged in a whisper. "You c-can kiss me."

"Fine." He planted a quick kiss on Lizzie's lips. "There? Happy?"

"Boo!" the aging actor heckled. "I've seen better kisses in community theater productions."

"Maybe we can find someone else to kiss her." Ashlyn's sly gaze slid over to Maxim.

Over my dead fucking body.

Without a second thought, he captured Lizzie's face in his hands, then slanted his mouth over hers. The moment their lips touched, he knew it was a mistake, but somehow, he couldn't stop himself. She had the softest, sweetest mouth he'd ever tasted, and the way she yielded to and melted into him sent his dominant instincts ablaze. His fingers slid into her lustrous locks, curling them around his fingers. When he gave a gentle tug, she moaned, her arousal tinging the air. His wolf howled in delight.

Dainty hands slid up his chest and clung to his shoulders like her life depended on it. Her mouth fully opened up to him, and he dipped his tongue inside to taste her. Kissing Lizzie was like drowning in the ocean, but never wanting to be rescued.

"Woohoo!" Ashlyn's piercing whoop yanked him back to reality, and he and Lizzie quickly broke apart.

"Someone get me a cigarette," the actor joked.

"Ew, I thought you said you quit ten years ago," his husband admonished.

"Yeah, but those two make me wanna fall off the wagon."

Lizzie's face was the color of her hair, and Wyatt couldn't blame her. He, too, was left heated from their kiss. His wolf, on the other hand, was all smug and satisfied, puffing its chest out in pride. Wyatt couldn't blame it either, especially when he spied the dark look on Maxim's face. It was almost as satisfying as punching it.

"*Oh-em-gee*, I'm definitely going to get a million views on that one!" Ashlynn cackled as she tapped on her phone.

Fuck! Wyatt ran his fingers through his hair. If that video got out—

"I—what the hell?" Ashlyn frantically swiped on the screen. "I can't find the video! Oh, and now my phone's going crazy." She shoved the phone at him. The screen showed a blue background and various bits of code running up and down. "Have you ever seen a phone do this?"

"Maybe you got a virus." From the corner of his eye, he spied Lizzie cover her mouth and her shoulders shake.

"Ack!" She dropped the device as if it literally had an infectious disease. "I need to get my extra phone! Don't do anything fun or juicy until I'm back," she shouted as she made a mad dash for the guesthouse.

"I suppose that was your handiwork?" he asked Lizzie when they were alone.

"Hey, she handed me her phone during dinner to show me all the matches she made on her dating app." The corner of her mouth tugged up. "Her phone loves making new friends and was only too happy to connect to my smartwatch.

In fact, it hardly had any security on it. I'm surprised her nudes haven't been leaked yet."

"Thank you for doing that," he said.

"Of course. We can't have anyone else seeing us ki—" She sucked in a breath. "D-doing that."

"Right." He cleared his throat. "Are you—"

"Oh!" She snapped her fingers. "I just remembered, I promised my dad I would check on something for him," she blurted out. Her hands slid down to her skirt. "My phone! Oh crap, it must have fallen out of my pocket. I'm gonna check the dining room or ask the staff." Without another word, she scampered off.

Wyatt fought the urge to go after her and instead remained still as a rock rooted to the floor like a tree. A cool breeze swept by, carrying with it the salty ocean air, clearing his senses of Lizzie's lingering scent and feel. But even when he wasn't in her presence, all he could think of, smell, and now, taste, was Lizzie.

How he would survive until Sunday, he didn't know. He might not even make it through the night.

Chapter Seven

Lizzie dashed toward the main house and up to the dining room where she found her phone in the chair she'd previously occupied. Slipping it into her pocket, she spun on her heel, intending to go back to the party, but the little flip her stomach executed made her halt.

Oh God.

OhGodohGod.

She added a couple more *oh Gods* in there, because right now, she could surely use an intercession from whatever higher being was listening.

Someway, somehow, she had to figure out what the *hell* was happening with her.

This entire week leading up to this, she'd been a ball of anxiety, thinking about having sex with Maxim and possibly disappointing him. At some point, she even wondered if it was possible to find someone to teach her, but there likely wouldn't be enough time to learn it all. Besides, from what her cousins had told her about dating on the apps as a woman, she'd probably end up swearing off technology altogether.

She really should be focusing on Maxim, yet each time he looked at her, or even came close to her, there was something about him that made her flinch away. Her wolf, too, was repulsed at the sight and smell of him.

Wyatt, on the other hand, well ... he had only to look at her, and she turned into a puddle.

Then that kiss happened.

Lord help her, now every fiber of her being was screaming for Wyatt Creed. His firm mouth. His hands. His hard body pressed up against hers.

Why did he have to go and kiss her?

And why did she have to like it so much?

She liked it so much, in fact, that she had Eames send her a copy of the video before obliterating the file from Ashlyn's phone.

This was crazy. She liked *Maxim*. This was why Wyatt was here in the first place, why they had this pretend dating scheme.

He didn't even want to kiss you in the beginning, she reminded herself. Indeed, she too had been apprehensive at the thought and agreed to it because she didn't want to blow their cover. That first peck had sent a tiny thrill through her, but the second one had scorched her panties off.

And now she had to go back out there and pretend everything was normal, like it had been before that soul-searing kiss.

She pressed her thighs together, hoping to relieve the pressure building between them. However, that only made it worse, as a shiver ran through her. Her nipples tightened as she remembered the way he tugged at her scalp.

All the gods in heaven, she was going to have to find the courage to face him after that. But first, she needed to calm her raging hormones down.

"Lizzie? Are you all right?"

She whirled around and saw a familiar figure ascending the stairs. "Maxim! What are you doing here?"

"It's my house?"

She clucked her tongue and pointed at him. "Right. Um, I left my phone here and went to grab it."

"I see." He stalked toward her. "I saw you running into the house. Are you sure you weren't nosing around?"

"What? Me? No," she said defensively.

"I was just teasing, don't worry." He flashed her a smile.

Though Lizzie was usually ecstatic to receive one of his signature smiles, this one felt oddly ... flat. "How about you? Shouldn't you be out there with your guests?"

"Yes, but it seems we've run out of wine, and so I volunteered to retrieve some."

"Why doesn't Eduardo or one of your staff do it?"

"This rare vintage I bought from an auction just arrived, so I thought since we're celebrating my new home, why not? However, I keep my most expensive bottles locked away in my cellar, and only I know the combination to the security system."

"I see."

He leaned toward her. "Do you want to see it?"

"The security system?"

"That too, I suppose." He chuckled. "And my wine cellar. It's underground."

"Oh, cool. Yeah, why not?" *Maxim actually wants to spend time with me.* And they might even be alone. Her wolf, however, did not appreciate the idea. No, it did not want to be around this male. Instead, it sought out the scent of vanilla, leather, burnt paper, and cherries. "Lead the way," she said firmly, ignoring her animal.

"Sure."

They headed downstairs and toward the kitchen, then through a door that led down another set of stairs.

"It's like a cave in here." The stone walls were cool under Lizzie's palms as she used them to guide her down the dimly-lit cellar.

"I saw this in a castle in France and had my architects recreate it." The walls were filled with racks of bottles from floor to ceiling. "Everything is kept at an exact temperature, plus, I have the best emergency fire system, should anything happen." He led her toward the end, where one section was separated by a glass door. "Bullet proof, and if the alarm goes off, a steel door will come down from above."

"All this for alcohol?"

"There's probably, oh, about a million dollars' worth of alcohol behind that glass."

"Wow, I didn't know wine could cost that much." She whistled low. "If you want, I know a place where you could get some great wine for two bucks."

"Thanks, I'll keep that in mind." There was a hint of irritation in his tone. "Lizzie, I wanted to ask you something."

"Hmmm?" She had already walked toward the control panel on the side, wondering what kind of system he had in place. Her fingers itched to touch the keypad.

"Are things okay with you and Wyatt?"

Now, that caught her attention. She whirled around to face him. "What do you mean?"

"I have eyes you know," he began. "And I've been observing you two."

"Oh?"

"Yes. You don't act like normal couples do."

She resisted the urge to yell, *did you not see that kiss,* at him. "Oh? And how are normal couples supposed to act?"

"I'm sorry if you're offended." He held his hands up. "I don't mean to pry. I'm just wondering how serious things are between the two of you. And if he gives you what you need and want."

Technically the answer was no, if he was talking about what she thought he was talking about. However, the thought of *that* made her all flustered. "Maxim ..."

"You're all flushed." He reached out to brush a lock of hair away from her face, his fingers brushing against her cheek. "I was just wondering, all those times we've bumped into each other, if I'd read you wrong."

All those times? What the heck was he talking about?

"I can tell when a woman is flirting with me, I just try not to encourage it especially if business is involved."

Her cheeks heated even more. "I—"

Maxim advanced toward her, crowding her in, one hand landing on the stone just above her to essentially trap her. She had no choice but to press up against the wall. Well, her other choice was to turn into her Lycan form and rake her claws down his face, which her inner wolf was itching to do. It bared its teeth at this bold male daring to invade their space.

"Maxim ..."

"Was I wrong?" He leaned in closer. "Weren't you trying to flirt with me at the office and at the magazine party?"

Hey! You seem tense! a disembodied voice said. *Whatsa matter, girly?*

What—oh. She was not just pressed up against the wall, but rather, her back was right up against the console that controlled the alarm. *Hey there.*

You in some kinda trouble? For some reason, to Lizzie, the alarm system sounded like an old man, kinda like a sweet old grandpa.

Yeah, I'm not in a good place right now. I need to get outta here.

You need a quick escape, girly? A distraction, maybe?

Yes, please.

Coming right up.

Maxim's lips were now inches from hers. "Lizzie, I need to confess something—what the *fuck?*" he cursed when an alarm blared, filling the room with a deafening sound. Something heavy slammed on the floors, sending a strong shockwave that had Maxim staggering away.

"Lizzie?"

Then, it started to rain water down on them, and when Lizzie looked up to the source, she saw that the sprinkler system had been activated.

That good enough of a distraction, girly?

It is! Thanks so much! she told the alarm system before she ran past Maxim and headed up the stairs, taking them two at a time. Upon reaching the top, she hurled herself right out the door—and straight into something solid and heavy.

"Lizzie?"

The familiar comforting scent and strong arms were

enough to calm down her frazzled nerves. "Wyatt?" Plastered against his chest, she stared up into his gorgeous hazel eyes, mesmerized by the bright green flecks.

"You didn't come back to the party, so I was worried." Frown lines appeared on his forehead. "Where did you—"

"Lizzie, wait!" Maxim shouted as he emerged from the cellar, clearly out of breath. "I—Hey, Wyatt." He swallowed a gulp of air.

Hazel eyes blazed as Wyatt's expression shifted from concern to murderous. "What the hell is happening here?" His gaze darted from Lizzie to Maxim. "Why are you both wet? Where did you come from?"

A knot formed in Lizzie's throat. "I can explain—"

"I was simply showing Lizzie my wine cellar when the alarm went off." Maxim brushed off an imaginary piece of lint from his wet shirt. "Completely accidental. I should call my alarm company and have them check if there's a bug."

"You do that," Wyatt muttered. "In the meantime, let's get you out of those wet clothes, Lizzie, before you catch a cold."

"I can't get a cold—hey!" Wyatt hooked his arm through hers and practically dragged her away. "Slow down, Wyatt! Short legs, short legs!"

He slowed his pace, but not by much. Lizzie could see and feel the tension from him, and by the time they made it to their room, he looked ready to burst.

She disentangled her arm from him as soon as they were inside. "I swear, Wyatt, I didn't want him to—"

"Didn't want him to what?" he roared as he spun around to face her. "So, he did touch you? Kiss you?"

"What? No! And what does it matter if he did?" And also

—why did she feel like she'd been caught doing something bad?

"Because you're mi—my girlfriend. At least, he thinks you're my girlfriend," he huffed. "The fact that he would try something while we're still committed makes my stomach turn, and you should be concerned too, if you've got your sights set on him."

"Why?"

"Ever heard the saying, 'if he cheats with you, he'll cheat on you'?"

"Maxim isn't like that," she retorted, which was met with a derisive snort. Okay, so maybe she didn't know that. "In any case, that's why we're here right? So I can be with him?"

His expression shifted into an emotion Lizzie couldn't quite name, but her inner alarm bells went off, crying *Danger! Danger!*

"Is it, Lizzie? Is that what you really want?"

"I—" She gulped. "Yes."

"Then why do you flinch away from him? Why do you look so uncomfortable when he looks at you or pays attention to you?"

"What?"

"I'm not blind, Lizzie," he said firmly. "Maybe you don't really want to be with him."

"What?" she shouted. "Yes, I do."

"The truth, Lizzie." He crossed his arms over his chest. "Now, or you can forget about this whole fake dating plan."

"I just ... I don't ..." *Argh! Why was this so hard?*

Wyatt brushed past her and reached for the door. "Bye, Li—"

"No!" Desperation clawed at her as she took hold of his forearm and pulled. "It's not what you think!"

"Then, what is it?"

"I've never had sex!" Holy fuck, she really said that aloud. *Stupid Wyatt!* "There, I said it. My deepest, darkest secret that no one knows about. Are you happy now?" He didn't say anything, he didn't even move. "Wyatt?" She shook his arm.

Slowly, Wyatt's body turned to her. "Are you serious?" His voice was a low whisper.

"Y-yes."

"Why?"

"Why what? Why haven't I had sex?"

A pulse ticked in his jaw. "Yeah."

"I just ... it's not been a priority, okay? I just ... I have my reasons." She released his arm. "So, excuse me if I'm not exactly comfortable having a man pay attention to me." Well, there was one time she was—that kiss earlier with him. "I just ... Oh *God*." Trudging over to the living room, she plastered herself on top of the plush love seat. "This is so embarrassing."

"Hey ... er, I'm sorry." The low dipping of the cushions beside her told her Wyatt had sat down too. "For forcing you to tell me your secret."

"You couldn't guess from my awkwardness around men and the fact that I had to get a fake boyfriend to get a real boyfriend?" God, he must think she was such a loser, especially since if she recalled correctly, she was about two years older than him.

"Everyone does things in their own time." His voice was

curiously assuring. "But I mean ... there's been no one? All this time?"

"I've been kissed and all, but there just hasn't been any chance."

"Not at school? College?"

"Ha! I wish."

"You said you've slept next to someone before."

"I meant like Mom or my cousins, Charley and Olivia, when we were kids," She didn't think he would think that she had meant another man.

"And so, you want your first time to be with Maxim?" There was an edge to his voice that made the hair on the back of her neck stand on end.

Sitting up, she said, "I wanted to have my first normal experiences with a man to be with Maxim. You know, like going on dates, snuggling on the couch on a rainy day, weekend getaways, and even mundane things like brunch on Sundays or attending family events."

"You want to marry him then?" his voice had gone hoarse.

"N-not exactly." Turning to him, she began to explain. "I didn't grow up like a normal kid. I skipped grades because regular schoolwork bored me to tears. I was doing advanced calculus by the time I was ten, and so my dad homeschooled me. Mom insisted I at least get the normal college experience like she did, so they enrolled me when I was fifteen. Didn't make it a whole year, and so I decided I would just work at Lone Wolf."

"I didn't know." Wyatt's eyes widened as his jaw slackened.

Oh God, now he does think I was some kind of loser.

"That's Goddamned impressive, Lizzie," he said. "You shouldn't be ashamed of that or think of yourself any less just because you didn't hit the milestones other people think you should have."

He was ... impressed? Her heart did a little flutter. "I know but ... you ever get this feeling that life just passed you by? Like, maybe there were things you didn't even know you wanted. And then shit happens that remind you that you're not really on this earth for too long, so you better do what you want."

"You're talking about the mages," he said in a quiet tone, as if he understood exactly what she was talking about. And why wouldn't he? He, too, had the same traumatizing experience.

"Yeah, you get it. And I want all those things. The house in the suburbs, the two-point-five kids, the dog. And whether or not that's with Maxim, I don't know yet, but I need to find out before I get thrown into another life and death situation and things don't end well."

"I would never let anything happen to you," he interrupted, then cleared his throat. "Nor will my father or the Alpha. To anyone."

"Thanks." She patted his hand. "But yeah, so if I'm a little tense around Maxim, it's because I just don't know anything about sex, and he must have tons of experience. I don't want to turn him off or disappoint him. I mean, I know the mechanics and, uh, I've done research." Heat flowed back into her face at the admission. "But the real thing ... it's not like I can get someone to teach that to me." She laughed nervously. "I mean, can I?"

"What?"

"Teach me. Sex." When she turned to him and their gazes crashed, she felt that sensation between her legs again, and her nipples turned hard as rocks. Her eyes lowered to his firm lips. "Wyatt ... would it be possible ... do you think ..."

"No!" He shot up to his feet. "Absolutely not."

She shoved her deeply wounded pride deep inside, locked it in a box, dumped it into the Pacific Ocean, and threw away the key. It would be the only way she could stop parading it around for anyone to stomp on. "You're absolutely right. Besides, Bastian's probably busy."

"What?" His shout reverberated throughout the room, and Lizzie swore the walls shook from the force of his voice. "What the fuck are you talking about?"

"I was wondering if Bastian would agree to teach me what I need to know to seduce Maxim." She blinked at him. "What did you think I meant?"

His fists clenched and unclenched at his sides. "I—nothing." Shoving his hands in his pockets, he turned away from her. "I need to make a call."

Lizzie let out a long, dramatic yawn. "And I think I'm gonna head to bed. 'Night, Wyatt." Despite her heart racing harder than a prized horse at the Kentucky Derby, she managed to make it to the bedroom, threw herself onto the bed, then let out a silent scream into the pillows.

You're an idiot, Elizabeth Eowyn Martin!

What made her even think Wyatt would want to have sex with her? Just because he gave her the kiss of her lifetime—which she had to admit, she didn't have much to compare to—it didn't mean a thing.

He's probably kissed a dozen, maybe hundreds of women that way.

The image of Wyatt kissing another woman made her chest ache and her wolf wanted to tear those imaginary women to bits.

Sighing, she crawled out of bed and padded toward the dressing room, where she began to get ready for sleep. *Good save though, with the Bastian thing.*

And if she found a tiny bit of satisfaction from seeing the expression on his face when she suggested she was going to sleep with his brother, well, who could blame her, after that big blow to her ego?

Nervously, she checked the bedroom before tiptoeing out, lest Wyatt was already in bed. *Their one bed*, she reminded herself. Oh God, talk about awkward.

Slipping between the covers, she turned off the lamp on the nightstand. Maybe she'd be lucky and he'll think she was asleep by the time he was ready for bed.

Or maybe, the earth would swallow her up, and she'd never have to face him again.

Chapter Eight

They say be careful what you wish for, and Lizzie soon learned how true that was the very next morning.

A knock on the door had her bolting upright.

"Wha—who—" A quick glance around reminded her where she was and what happened the previous night. Turning to the other side of the bed, the unruffled covers made a pit form in her stomach.

Where was Wyatt?

Throwing the duvet aside, she quickly headed to the living area to answer the door. "Hello? Oh, hey, Eduardo."

"Good morning, Miss Martin," the butler greeted. "How was your sleep?"

"Surprisingly good." She never had a problem falling asleep. It was almost a skill. "Um, can I help you?"

"I just came by to inform you of a few things, Miss Martin," he began. "Breakfast is laid out downstairs, or I can have something sent up if you wish to dine alone."

"Sounds great. Is Wyatt taking his breakfast downstairs?"

"That's why I came to see you. He just left."

"Left?" She didn't mean to shout at him; the idea just shocked her. "Sorry. I mean ... did he say why?"

"Emergency at work, apparently. Mr. Silver suddenly had to leave for New York too, so he rode with him on his plane. Mr. Creed sends his apologies, but he didn't want to disturb you. He says his jet will be available to take you back to New York at your scheduled departure time, though if you wished to leave earlier, just inform me, and I'll call the captain to see what arrangements can be made. What would you like me to do?"

"Um, yeah let me think about this and get back to you."

"As you wish."

Once Eduardo left, Lizzie ambled back to the bedroom. Aside from his section of the bed being left undisturbed, there were no other signs that he had gone. Even his things were still in the dressing area.

So, Wyatt just up and left her here. Alone.

Asshole.

She crossed her arms over her chest. *Fine.* Obviously, he was sending her a message. He didn't want to play her fake boyfriend anymore. She understood loud and clear. Maybe it was time they did break up. Maxim almost kissed her last night. He already suspected their relationship was on the rocks. Perhaps when she signaled that she and Wyatt were done, Maxim would make his move. *Too bad he left with the asshole.*

No way was she was getting back on his plane though. "Eames, book me the first available flight back to New York, please. Then have a car come pick me up in fifteen minutes."

Of course, Lizzie.

Since she didn't bring a lot of stuff, Lizzie packed all her things in no time. She also managed to sneak out of the house and into her rideshare car without running into anyone,

Unfortunately, the only flight Eames could get her had one stopover in Atlanta, and that plane was delayed, so she ended up spending a couple of hours at Hartsfield-Jackson. By the time she landed in LaGuardia, it was six in the evening, hours after when she would have landed had she taken the private jet. She tried not to think about it, because she was still pretty furious at Wyatt for leaving without a word.

Lizzie, you have an urgent message from your father, Eames said as soon as she was at baggage claim and he was connected her cell network.

"What?" She checked her phone. "Huh." Completely dead. It must have run out of batteries hours ago. "Ask him what's wrong."

One moment. A few second passed. *I'm re-routing his call now.*

"Lizzie, where the hell are you?" Her father's voice burst through the tiny speakers on the side of her smartwatch. "I've been trying to call you."

"My flight was delayed and my phone must have run out of batteries. Just landed in LaGuardia a couple minutes ago."

"Flight? Where did you go?"

"Uh, long story, Pops. So, what's up?"

He blew out a breath. "Another breach. This time at Creed."

"Creed?" Her thoughts immediately turned to Wyatt. "What happened?"

"Still trying to figure it out. But they were attacked at

multiple points. The office and Sebastian's home network, too. Even Jade's work computer. The dragon's pretty furious."

"Are you at Lone Wolf or Creed? I can grab a ride to wherever you are."

"We're fine, but can you check on Wyatt's home network? No one can seem to contact him either, so might be best to make sure he's okay. Bastian's been alerted, but he says everything's fine on his end."

Of course she would have to go see Wyatt. "All right, let him know I'm on my way."

"Thanks, I'll talk to you soon."

Lizzie huffed. *It's okay, I'm a professional*, she told herself. "Eames?"

Car's already on the way.

"You're a gem as always." Grabbing her bag, she proceeded out to the curb, and soon, her car arrived.

Her anxiety grew as she neared Manhattan. She didn't know where Wyatt lived exactly, maybe Dad had sent Eames the address, though she was not at all surprised when the car stopped in front of an elegant building on the Upper East Side. The uniformed doorman smiled at her as he opened the door. As she expected, the inside was done up in warm wood tones, decorated with fine objets d'art, and plush carpets. The kind of snooty place she hated, where the residents would likely turn their noses up at her, or worse, think she was there to deliver their dinner.

Geez, it even smelled old.

"Miss?" The man standing behind the front desk called out to her as she made her way to the elevators. "Can I help you?"

His tone was polite, but the meaning was there. She did

not belong here. Too bad she couldn't hack into the concierge so she could just break into Wyatt's home and not have to worry about running into him.

"I'm here to see—Wyatt?"

Sure enough, he was walking through the entrance, phone to his ear. "I don't fucking care how you do it, just find her! I—" He halted in his tracks as soon as their gazes crashed into each other. Relief crossed his face. "Lizzie? You're here?"

"Uh, hey."

"Where the hell have you been?" He reached her in a split second, hands gripping her arms as if to ensure she was really there. "When Henry said you didn't show up for the flight, I thought something had happened to you."

A tiny spark of warmth lit up in her chest. He'd been worried about her? "Uh, no time for that now. Your home network might have been compromised. I need to go check it."

A serious expression settled on his face. "All right, let's go."

She followed him to the elevator. He pressed the button marked *P*, and soon, they reached his floor. It literally was his floor because the doors opened up right into a foyer that led into a massive apartment.

"The router's through here," he said gesturing for her to follow him across the living area and through a door on the right into what was probably his home office. Walking over to an antique glass-fronted bookshelf behind the desk, he opened one of the doors.

"Inside." The modem and router were cleverly hidden inside, perhaps to preserve the old world feel of the room.

"Did you turn your computer on today?" She nodded at the PC monitor on the desk.

"No, not yet. When I got home this morning, I just unpacked and—" He stopped short.

"And what?" She turned to him, planting her hands on her hips.

"I went to the office."

"All right. Thanks," she said, then sat down on the hard-wood floor and went to work. "Hey there, what's up?" she asked the modem, placing her hands on the black box.

Whoah! Duuuude. The modem sounded like a teenage boy. *You can talk?*

Normally she didn't mind chitchat, but they were in a time crunch here. "Yeah, long story. I promise I'll tell you all about it, but I'm just worried someone might have tried to hack into you."

Hack into me? How?

"That's what I'm here to find out. Have you had any unusual pings? Did any devices you don't recognize try to access you? Any other unusual activities?"

Hmmm, let me think. It paused, the lights on the side moving in a rhythmic pattern. *Nope, just me and my usual buds around here.*

"Awesome. Let me check on them just in case." She moved over to the router and asked it the same questions, who confirmed there was nothing out of the ordinary. The PC, too, didn't recognize any other type of access. Still, just to make sure, she took out Angie from her backpack and connected it to the modem, then added a couple of extra security protocols and firewalls, plus instructed it to alert her if it was breached at any time. When she was done, she instructed Eames to tell her dad her progress as her phone remained dead in her pocket.

Getting up, she addressed Wyatt. "What other devices do you have here that are connected to your network?"

"Just the PC," he said.

"That's it? No smart speakers, lights?"

He shook his head.

"Internet-connected fridge? Security system?"

"I have a security system. You've met them."

"I have?" She didn't recall seeing or touching any panels out in the living room.

"Yes, the staff downstairs."

She rolled her eyes. "Geez, you live like Luddite."

"I have a TV," he said defensively.

"Uh-huh." She smirked at him. "I suppose you still watch your shows via cable TV."

"I only need the news in the morning," he said.

"Then what do you do for entertainment?"

He pointed to the books on the shelves. "I read books."

"Like, the ones printed on paper?"

"How else?"

"Of course you would read real books." She shoved Angie back into her bag. "Okay, we're all good here."

"No breach?"

"None that I could detect. Didn't anyone tell you what was happening?"

He shook his head. "I was at the office getting through some paperwork. I like to shut everything down when I need to concentrate. But then I checked in with my pilot, and he said you didn't show up at the airstrip. I was ...worried about you."

She zipped up her backpack with a vicious pull. "I bought my own ticket."

"Why didn't you take the jet back?"

Her head snapped up, and she lifted an eyebrow at him, one that was meant to say, *You have to ask?* When he didn't respond, she slung the backpack over her shoulder, then brushed past him. "Everything looks good here. My dad will be by your office tomorrow to check on all your other devices. You can ask him any other questions."

She gave him a two-fingered salute before she walked out of the study, striding across the living room toward the elevators. She reached for the call button but was promptly blocked as Wyatt slipped between her and the doors.

"Did you need anything else checked?" *Like your brain?*

"I know you're mad at me for leaving you in Miami."

"*Ding, ding, ding*! Give the man a prize. Now, please, get out of my—*eep*!"

Wyatt moved so fast, she barely had time to react, and she found herself pressed up against the wall, his grip on her arms. Fury blazed in his light hazel eyes as they glowed with the presence of his wolf.

"Wyatt, calm down." She should be scared; Lycans never revealed their wolf side unless they meant to shift. But somehow, she wasn't afraid. In fact, the most delicious thrill zinged all the way down to her toes at the thought that his animal was so near the surface. Her she-wolf, too, rumbled with pleasure.

"Tell me you weren't serious about asking my brother to fuck you," he growled.

"W-w-hat?" She was distracted by the fact that his face

was centimeters away from hers as well as from his heady scent that enveloped her.

"What you said last night." His jaw tightened. "Tell me you weren't even considering him."

"I—of course not."

"No?"

She shook her head vigorously.

"Then why did you tell me you wanted to sleep with him?"

Her heart thudded against her chest so loudly, he could probably pick it up with his Lycan senses. "B-because ... I— are you going to make me say it?"

His hands tightened on her. "Why, Lizzie?"

"Because you already said no! Before I could even scrounge up enough courage to finish asking," she cried. "You barely wanted to be my fake boyfriend. You didn't want to kiss me either. Then I was going to ask you t-to help me, but you were already saying no before I could finish the question." It was too late now; the dam had broken, and she had to continue. "And you want to know the real truth? My pride can only be stomped on so many times before I lose my self-respect, Wyatt." Her chest constricted at the memory of being rejected by him. It felt a thousand times worse than when Maxim blew off her attempts at flirtation. "I wasn't going to let anyone else make me feel unwanted and unattractive, just because I'm a virgin."

"Unwanted? Unattractive?" He shouted as he released her. "You're joking, right?"

"Joking?"

"I ..." He scrubbed a hand down his face. "You're fucking

beautiful, Lizzie, as if you didn't know that. Maxim's a giant knob if he can't see that."

"Y-you think I'm beautiful?" That thought floored her.

"You are. And don't let anyone make you think otherwise. But I just couldn't risk getting emotions involved."

"So that's what this was all about? You're afraid I'm so inexperienced that I would develop feelings for you and I would get hurt when you let me down."

"Something like that."

"Ha!" She put her hands on her hips. "How presumptuous."

"It's a valid concern, it's not like it never happens," he pointed out. "Can you honestly say that getting hurt is out of the question? That it's an outcome of this experiment of yours that would one hundred percent, *never* happen?"

"It's certainly a valid result of such an experiment." There were no such things as one hundred percent guarantees, after all. "But then, I'll never know unless I perform the experiment, will I? I just need to find a willing subject."

A strangled sound ripped from his throat. Straightening his shoulders, he leaned over to her. "If we do this, we can't get our emotions involved. Not just for personal reasons, but to protect our working relationship."

Why the hell didn't he bring that *very valid* concern up in the first place? She at least wouldn't have felt like she'd been outright rejected. "What am I? Some teenage girl with stars in her eyes? For God's sake, Wyatt, I'm about fifteen years past puberty. Besides, I just want this out of the way before I go and seduce Maxim."

His lips tightened. "Why did you want to ask me in the

first place? Because I was convenient? Would you have asked Bastian next? Or maybe some random—"

"For crying out loud, Wyatt." She threw her hands up. Was she going to have to go through this with every man she propositioned? "Why all the questions? With all the fuss you're making, you'd think *I* was the one taking *your* virtue."

"What am I to you then? A piece of meat?"

"I thought you were the one who was afraid of emotions being involved."

He blew out a breath. "It's one thing to mutually agree on a no strings attached arrangement, and quite another to use someone like a body as if there was no person attached to it."

She opened her mouth to make some smart retort, but shut it quickly.

He was absolutely correct.

And he had every right to question her motives. God, she felt like the shittiest person in the world. "I-I apologize, Wyatt," she began, lowering her gaze. "A-and you're not j-just a body to me."

"What am I to you?" The air around them grew thick. "Why do you want to do this with me?"

Slowly, she lifted her head to meet his light gaze. "Y-you make me feel safe, Wyatt. I c-can't explain why." The way those eyes bore into her made her tremble. "You just do. And I know at the end of the day, after all this, you're the kind of person who would respect me." Her heart thrummed so fast, she thought it would eventually make its way out of her chest.

"Lizzie ..."

She couldn't bear to look at him, so she closed her eyes. His large, calloused palm enveloped her cheek, and his warm breath tickled her ear. "I will always respect you, Lizzie. No matter what. If you doubt anything else, believe in that."

"I do believe you. So, can we agree on just this one time? And no emotions involved?"

He nodded, the scrape of his bristly jaw on her skin sent a thrill down to her core. "No regrets or awkwardness when it's done."

"Agreed. And we respect each other during a-and after."

"Agreed."

"So ... yes?"

"Yes," he answered before he devoured her mouth with his.

Lizzie had no choice but to open to his claiming mouth. She only had a taste of his tongue last night, but now he invaded her completely, tasting—no, consuming her, like she was his last meal. Her hands braced against his chest, clinging to him as if he was the only thing stopping her from falling into an endless abyss.

He angled his mouth the opposite way, and slowed down. She couldn't quite explain it, but it was like a whole new experience. The deliberate strokes of his tongue built up the tension in her core, and soon she was panting and rubbing herself against him.

"Please, Wyatt," she said, not really sure what she was asking.

He let out a grunt and released her. "Bedroom?"

"Yes."

He practically dragged her across the room, up the stairs to the second floor, and down a hallway and into what she guessed was the master bedroom.

"Sit on the edge of the bed," he ordered.

The dominance in his voice made her shiver, and it was a wonder she somehow managed to walk over to the large, king-sized bed in the middle. She did as he ordered and sat on the end of the mattress.

Wyatt had remained by the doorway, watching her. Slowly, he stalked toward her, unbuttoning his white shirt, revealing his muscled chest and chiseled abs. She'd seen it before after he shifted back into his human form, but she'd been so concerned about the bullet holes all over him, she didn't have time to admire his body. He shrugged off the shirt, and let it drop to the floor, then popped two buttons on his jeans. He continued to make his way to her until he was between her parted knees.

"You've had an orgasm before, right?"

She nodded. "I have toys."

"Good."

"Good?" She blinked. "Why is that important if I'm learning about sex?"

"First lesson: a woman should know how to give herself pleasure," he began. "To know her own body and never settle for less than what she wants."

Her eyes bugged out when he lowered himself to his knees. "Wh-what part of the l-lesson is this?"

"The second." His hands pushed the skirt of her sundress up to her thighs. "A woman should know how to receive pleasure."

"Wyatt, how is this—" The protest died in her throat when his lips touched the inside of her thigh, sending an electric shock straight up her core. "Wyatt ..."

"You smell incredible, Lizzie," he murmured against her skin. "You're wet, I can tell." She saw one hand slip down to his pants and disappear under the fabric. "God, you make me hard with just this delicious smell."

Holy moly, seeing him on his knees, stroking himself while he kissed her thighs drenched her panties further.

"Please, Lizzie. Let me taste you?"

"Yes," she moaned, practically thrusting her hips at him. "I want you to."

He needed no further instruction as he shoved his face into her. She let out a squeal when his tongue licked at her drenched, probably already see-through white cotton panties. "Ooooh!" He lapped at her slow and deliberately, the tip teasing her slit, barely touching the bundle of nerves at the top. Her body tensed, the feeling building up inside her, but she let out a whimper when he stopped.

"Why did you—?" The ripping of fabric was her answer. He had torn her panties away.

"Look at me, Lizzie," he commanded.

Her head lowered, cheeks heating at the sight of him between her thighs, naked to his gaze. Those hazel eyes blazed again, the pupils blowing up right before he pressed his mouth to her nether lips. The urge to close her legs was strong, but his grip was stronger. He kept her spread as he feasted on her, teasing her mercilessly with his flicks and licks and noisy slurps. It was indecent, and a huge turn on, the way he enjoyed eating her out so much.

"Wyatt," she gasped. "I don't know ... what to do."

"Whatever you ... feel ... like," he said between laps.

"I ..." Her fingers itched to grasp his hair, and so she did. When she raked her nails down his scalp, he let out a strangled moan. So, she grabbed a handful and tugged, and he made the most erotic groan. Then, as if to pay her back, he moved his mouth higher, his tongue flicking out to tease her clit.

She would have jumped off the bed had his hands not held her down.

"Easy," he said. "Relax. Do you want to lie back?"

"Th-that might help."

He assisted her in moving up the bed, so she lay flat on her back, feet planted on the mattress. Once she was relaxed, he crawled between her legs once more. "Don't be so tense," he whispered. A hand stroked her lower belly, making her unclench, then inched down. "That's it." His fingers teased her furred mound, then slipped down to stroke her drenched slit. "So wet, my Lizzie."

She closed her eyes, letting the low baritone of his voice caress her the way his fingers were teasing her pussy.

"Do you use your fingers inside?"

"S-sometimes."

He dipped the tip inside her. "And other toys?"

She nodded. "You won't have to worry about hurting me."

Gently, he probed one finger into her. "Gorgeous. I love the way your pussy sucks me right in."

She gasped.

"Do you like the dirty talk? Be honest. I promise I won't think less of you." He pushed the finger deeper in. "I just need to know what turns you on. What you like and don't like."

This was part of the lesson, she told herself. "Mm-hmmm. I ... like it."

"If there's something you don't like me saying, just tell me, and I'll stop."

"Don't ... stop ... that." She pushed her hips against his hand. "Please."

"My Lizzie ..." He lowered his head to place his tongue on her clit again. "Your clit is so sensitive. I can feel your pussy get wetter. Fuck, my hand is getting drenched."

"Oh, I like that!" she said enthusiastically. "Definitely do more of that."

His shoulders shook. "Aye, aye, captain."

"Did you just make another jo—ooohhh!" He sucked hard at her clit and thrust his finger into her at the same time.

Oh God, oh God, oh God!

The orgasm came out of nowhere, punching its way through her like it had no place else to go. Her body shuddered, her feet stamping on the bed as pleasure rocked her. Wyatt kept on eating her out her like a champ, his tongue and mouth like a machine that never ran out of steam. Suffice to say, she was a hot, shaking mess by the time he raised himself up on his elbows to look up at her, the biggest grin on his face.

"What, that good?"

"I'll tell you when I find my brain." Good Lord, she'd never had an orgasm like that. She closed her eyes and took deep breaths, willing the oxygen back into her system. When she recovered, she said, "What's next?"

"What do you want to do?" He took her hand and pulled her upright to her knees. "I can always give you another orgasm."

"How nice of you." She gave him a quick peck on the cheek. "But now I want to make you feel good." Her hand moved down over his rock-hard abs, and toward his pants, but he caught her wrist. "Wyatt?"

"Hold on, that's quite an advanced lesson."

"I can handle it."

He lifted her hand up and kissed her palm. "I've no doubt. But you need to learn to walk before you fly. Lizzie, despite what you might see in movies or read in magazines, a man's pleasure can start in the brain, too."

"How?"

"Use the other senses aside from touch. Try one of those first."

"How?"

He leaned back on his heels. "Why don't you think it over." As if to give her a clue, his gaze lowered to her chest.

"Oh, I get it." He wanted to *see* her naked. A blush heated her all over. *Get over it, Lizzie,* she told herself. *If you want to have sex, you gotta get used to being naked around a man.*

Reaching across her chest, she tugged down the strap of her sundress, leaving one shoulder bare.

"Good start," he commended. "Go on."

Encouraged, she did the same to the other strap, then pulled the torso down to her waist to reveal her white strapless bra.

"God, you're beautiful." His eyes lowered to her chest. "You have the most amazing breasts. Big and luscious. I bet they're more than a handful."

Reaching behind her, she unhooked the bra. A wave of shyness washed over her, and she kept her arms around herself. *You can do this.* Slowly, she lowered her arms.

"Mother ..." Wyatt sucked in a breath. "Your nipples are incredible. So pink and large." He tugged his pants off, leaving him only in his underwear, then he palmed the significant bulge of his cock. "More."

Feeling bold, she crawled toward him, discarding her bra and dress along the way. Lifting one breast up, she directed the tip toward his face. Needing no further encouragement, he captured one nipple between his lips.

Taste.

The sensation of his mouth on her nipples was nothing like she'd ever felt before. There was something so deeply erotic about the way he admired and worshipped her. "Wyatt ... so good."

"Tell me more," he urged, pausing briefly before flicking a tongue at her hardened nipple.

Hearing.

"Your mouth is so talented. You made me come so fast when you ate my pussy. Suck my nipples harder, please." He did so, then shifted her body so she straddled him. His erection pressed up right against her bare lips, and she rubbed her hips up and down, shuddering as her clit hit the ridge of his cock through his underwear.

Smell was the last sense, but she wasn't sure how to tease him with it. Well, there was one way, at least for Lycans. Bringing her wrists up to the side of his head, she rubbed the inside of them against his cheek and down his neck. Scent-marking was an intimate gesture among Lycans, a way to leave your scent on someone else and mark them as yours.

He let out a deep growl, then before she knew it, she was on her back, and Wyatt was on top of her. He kissed her savagely, like a wild animal, and she loved it. In response, she raked her nails down his back. She wanted to howl in delight as it only seemed to drive him even crazier.

"Are you ready?" he panted against her mouth when he managed to pull away. "You can still say no."

Never. "I'm ready. I want you so bad, Wyatt."

Grunting, he briefly left her to reach for something in his bedside table. *A condom.* She appreciated the gesture, but they were Lycans, and they didn't get any STDs, and getting pregnant was very rare. "You don't have to," she said. "You know we're safe, right?"

"I know, but on the off chance ..."

"Right." It was his boundary, and she was willing to stay within it. *I should learn how to use one anyway.*

He ripped the foil with his teeth, then took out the rubber ring, tugged his briefs off and pulled it on his— "Holy moly!"

"Lizzie?" He paused, frowning. "What's the matter."

She gulped. "Er, nothing." Her eyes nearly popped out of her eye sockets. "It's just ... none of my toys are, uh, that big." She never really cared for the realistic toys, but maybe she should have ordered at least one. But then, how was she supposed to know she'd have her first time with King Dong over here?

"We'll take it slow." She didn't miss the slight tug at the corner of his mouth. "And if it does hurt, we'll stop."

"O-okay." She lay back down under him, spreading her legs to accommodate him. "What should I do? Where do I put my hands?"

"Anywhere." He lowered his head and kissed her belly, then made his way up to her mouth. "Everywhere. Wherever you want."

He kissed her in that slow, deliberate way again before he aimed the tip of his cock at her entrance. The blunt tip slipped into her entrance, and he began to push.

Lizzie didn't know how to describe the sensation of Wyatt entering her. She felt so full and tight. There wasn't any pain, none that made her want to stop anyway, but it was just uncomfortable and difficult to move.

"Relax. Don't tense up."

She didn't even notice it, but her body went rigid. So, she loosened her muscles, allowing him to push in even more. After what seemed like eternity, he was fully inside her.

"God, Lizzie, you feel so good," he murmured against her cheek. "Fuck, I don't know how I'm gonna do this."

"Take your time," she said. "I'm not going anywhere. But will you kiss me some more?"

He captured her mouth again, pushing his tongue against hers in an erotic dance. She protested when he pulled his mouth away, but then he shifted lower to kiss her neck, and the most wonderful sensations shot straight to her core. His lips teased her, and his tongue licked at the sensitive skin under her ear. Then, a hand snaked down between them where their bodies met, and he began to stroke her clit. She moaned into his mouth, and her hips jerked forward involuntarily, causing the most incredible sensation deep within her. She did it again. And again. And again, and with each movement, pleasurable shocks zinged through her.

"You're getting wetter," he said. "Good. Now let me try ..." He slid out an inch, and then thrust back in. "Was that okay?"

"Y-yes."

He repeated the motion, and her body shuddered. "Yes?"

"Oh God ... that felt so good." She pushed her hips up at him. "More."

Bracing his hands on either side of her, he thrust in and out, going faster and faster each time. The sensation was too much, and there were too many things happening at the same time. His hands were all over her, his mouth on her breasts and nipples, then kissing her again. The pressure built inside her, growing and growing until there was nowhere to go.

"Wyatt!" Her body tensed, seizing up as wave after wave of pleasure washed over her. He continued to move in and out of her, working through her orgasm, pushing her to the edge until she had no choice but to fall.

She thought it was over when he pulled out, but he lifted one of her legs and twisted her around so she faced away from him. When she lay on her side, he grabbed her thigh and pulled her back, his cock thrusting into her from behind.

Oh God, how the hell did it feel different from this angle?

The feel of him was familiar, but the sensation of him dragging along inside of her was new. His cock seemed to hit other parts of her, like she had buttons for pleasure that could only be reached in this position. His other arm slid under her and wrapped around her waist, pulling her close to him as he continued to piston inside her until she reached another earth-shattering orgasm. When he pulled out, then moved on top of her again, all she could think of was, *good Lord, he wasn't done yet?*

Wyatt shoved her knees apart, then pushed two fingers inside her as he kissed and sucked on her nipples, coaxing another orgasm from her body before he spread her legs. Pulling her to him, he thrust into her again.

She grabbed onto his buttocks, scraping her nails into the flesh as he pummeled into her. It was too much. "Please ... oh please ..."

"One ... more ... my Lizzie," he urged. "You can do it."

"I ..." She fell—no leapt—off the edge as her pleasure burst through her. He let out a strangled cry as his thrusts became erratic, then his body convulsed. His cock twitched deep inside her, and he kept pushing and pushing, crying out her name over and over until he thrust all the way in one last time, bracing his forearms on either side of her to stop from crushing her. He groaned several times until his breathing slowed and his body relaxed. Giving her a kiss on the cheek, he pulled out and rolled onto his back beside her.

Lizzie was still plastered to the mattress, her body like jelly, boneless and unresponsive. There were still phantom shocks of pleasure moving throughout her, and she didn't dare move an inch, wanting them to last as long as possible.

A hand reached over to her, wrapping around her fingers. "Lizzie," Wyatt breathed as he lifted her hand to his mouth and planted a kiss there.

She managed to twist to her side to face him, meeting his gaze. The look on his face was something she'd never seen before. He looked calm as usual, but there was no coolness lying underneath. Warmth radiated through him as his mouth turned up into a smile that reached his eyes. It was reassuring, but unnerving at the same time. Arrogant, composed Wyatt, she knew and could handle. The man next to her, well, she didn't know what to make of him.

"Are you feeling okay?" he asked.

"Oh yes," she said. Her chest constricted because it dawned on her that this was it. Just one time, they agreed.

"Thank you, Wyatt." She crawled over to him, then pressed her lips to his temple. "You were wonderful and thoughtful and caring." She swallowed the lump growing in her throat, but she'd made a promise to him that there would be no emotions, no awkwardness or regrets. And mutual respect. "I couldn't have asked for a better first lover. I'll never forget this, and I hope it was good for you too. So, thank you." She glanced at him one last time, committing the picture of this Wyatt—relaxed, sated, and smiling—to memory as she might never see it again. "I should get going here." When he made a motion to get up, she waved him away. "No, no, get some rest. You deserve it." She forced a chuckle before turning away to slide off the bed.

"Lizzie ..."

She looked over her shoulder at him, but not before plastering a casual smile on her face. "Yes, Wyatt?"

His dark blond brows knitted together. "I ..." He cleared his throat. "You're welcome. And have a safe trip home."

"You betcha." She tsked and pointed at him. "I'll see you around."

"Yeah ..."

Quickly, she picked up her dress and shimmied into it, then headed outside. Her shoes lay by the elevator, so she slipped into them and picked up her backpack before calling the elevator.

The silence inside Wyatt's cavernous apartment was deafening as she listened for the signs of footsteps. But no, there were none. Wyatt wasn't coming after her.

Lizzie, your blood pressure has dropped, Eames said. *In fact, your vitals have been wildly erratic the past hour. Should I call a doctor?*

I'm all right, Eames. No need to call a doctor. Just a car, please.

Of course, Lizzie.

The loud ding indicated the elevator arrived. She waited for half a second before stepping inside. As the car descended, she wondered what would happen next time she saw him.

"Nothing," she answered herself. They would both be adults about it and act normal, like that life shattering event never happened. She could do it too. She would have to, because she and Wyatt had an agreement. This experiment could only have one outcome, and this would be it.

Chapter Nine

Wyatt lay unmoving on the bed, listening to the sound of Lizzie's footsteps as she walked across the hardwood floors, followed by the soft *ding* announcing the arrival of the elevators. The *swoosh* of the doors told him she was really gone.

It was all over and done.

Still, her intoxicating scent surrounded him—from the sheets, the traces of her on his body, and of course, where she marked him on his neck, right at his pulse where the smell would linger on.

With a furious growl, he bounded off the bed and stalked to the bathroom. He ripped off the condom and threw it into the trash, then hopped into the shower, turning it to the hottest setting. When he grabbed his washcloth to wash her scent away, his wolf yowled in protest. That only made him scrub harder, leaving his skin red and raw.

Of course, that didn't do much good as the moment he stepped out of his bathroom, the scent of sex and Lizzie invaded his nostrils. Fuming silently, he strode out to the living room, sat down on the couch, then reached over to his drink cart to pour himself a half glass of scotch.

Goddammit.

There was a reason he told her no the first time. It was one thing to play the part of her boyfriend, and another to teach her sex so she could be with another man. His stomach turned, and his throat felt like he'd swallowed thumbtacks at the thought that he'd practically handed Lizzie over to Maxim.

He took a sip of the scotch, then tipped the glass to guzzle it all the way down. The temporary warmth and buzz felt good, but thanks to his Lycan metabolism, it was gone in seconds. But even if he were human, he could never erase the memory of making love to Lizzie.

He'd already predicted this would happen, yet he did nothing to stop it. Leaving her back in Miami was only a temporary solution. The moment she'd walked into his den, he was a goner. And when she offered herself to him, not even the fires of hell could have made him say no a second time.

And she thought he'd been talking about her when he said he didn't want to get emotions involved.

He attempted to sleep on the couch, but he lay there completely awake for hours, eyes open as his thoughts tortured him with the memory of Lizzie, her skin, her smell, her lips. The soft sighs and moans she made when he touched her. The way she gripped him, so hot and tight—

He shot upright, then poured himself another half glass and knocked it back. The only thing he could do now was face the truth: Lizzie did not want him. It was Maxim Silver she wanted.

Wyatt supposed he should be used to being second best by now.

The urge to throw the glass against the wall was strong, but he resisted. *You're not an animal*, he reminded himself. He may share his body with one, but he was the one in control. His grandmother's voice rang in his head.

Never let that savage side of you out.

Control the vicious beast.

Tame your feral nature.

Before it could protest, he shut the beast out. He imagined putting it in a cage with steel walls. Completely contained. Unreachable.

The silence in his brain was deafening. But at least he could now sleep.

As the CEO of a billion-dollar security company with thousands of people depending on him not only for their livelihood and in some cases, safety, Wyatt could not afford to get distracted. His father entrusted this monolith he built from scratch to him, and there was no way he would run it to the ground.

So, he went through his busy day as he always did, taking calls, attending meetings, reading over contracts, and perusing paperwork. Whenever his thoughts would stray too far away, he would quickly shut it down. The temptation to think of Lizzie was too great, but he knew in time, he would train himself to forget her. For now, he would avoid her as best he could.

"Mr. Creed?" his assistant's voice burst through the

phone speaker. "You have a visitor. From Lone Wolf Investigations and Security."

Lone Wolf? His stomach flipped in excitement, but then he recalled Lizzie saying her father would be here to check on his devices after the breach.

He swallowed hard. He didn't know what was worse—facing Lizzie or her father after last night.

"Mr. Creed?"

"Send him in, Ryan." Rising from his chair, he walked over to the front of his desk and put his phone on top, along with his tablet, laptop, and even an old smartwatch. When he heard the door open, he turned to face Quinn Martin. "I have all my stuff here, and—" His heart careened into his ribcage as his gaze landed on the person entering his office. "Lizzie?"

"Uh, hey, Wyatt." She waved at him. Today, she wore a green sweater, a brown and white checkered pleated skirt, and suede knee-high boots. Her red hair was pulled back into a high ponytail, away from her beautiful face. "Dad was busy today, so he asked me to check on your stuff," she stated in a business-like voice.

"I see." He gestured to the table, ignoring the sweat building on his palms. "You told me to show you everything, so here they are."

"Great." She brushed past him and placed her backpack on the floor. "Hmmm, okay. Just sit tight and let me do my thing. Hello, naughty boy, we meet again."

"I beg your pardon?"

She lifted his tablet in the air. "You haven't been connecting to strange WiFi networks, have you?" Her brows knitted in concentration as he noticed they always did when having a conversation with any device. "That's my good boy."

She gave it a pat on the back before placing it back down on the table. She sat down on one of the chairs across his desk. Then, she took his laptop, crossed a thigh over the other, and balanced the device on her knees. "I need a hand," she said.

"What?"

"Your hand. For your fingerprint, I mean." She held a hand out. "Please?"

He offered her his hand, but she wrapped her palm around his forefinger instead, then pressed it to the security touchpad. He could have sworn she rubbed it lightly, but it was over much too soon to tell.

"Thanks." Once again, she placed her hands on the computer as she "spoke" to it.

Once she was done, she declared, "All good." She shut the laptop lid then put it back in the same spot. Reaching into her pocket, she produced a lollipop and unwrapped it. "Sorry, didn't have time for lunch, just need a little sugar rush." She gave it a lick before putting it in her mouth, then turned back to the rest of his devices.

Wyatt swallowed hard. The gesture had been so quick and had been over in a second, but it replayed in his mind, like a movie on slow motion. But with her back to him, he was unable to read if she did it intentionally or not.

Before he could figure it out, she picked up the smart-watch, then flashed him a sly smile. "Not quite a Luddite."

His heart jumped in his throat at the reminder of their conversation yesterday. "I haven't worn that in months."

Her finger rubbed the dust off the strap. "Why do you keep it then?"

"It was from my mother. A gift. I wore it for a while, but the damned thing was annoying, and so I stuck it in a drawer.

"Annoying? How?"

"Kept telling me to stand up and stretch, drink water, and get more sleep. It was like having a portable nagger."

"Ah, so like having your actual mom around?" Though filled with humor, the way those arctic blue eyes pierced into him and saw right through his soul was infuriating and unnerving.

He crossed his arms over his chest. "Are you done?"

"Almost."

She turned back and picked up his phone, but it slipped from her hand. "Oops!"

As she bent down to retrieve it, her skirt flipped up, and a flash of pink lace panties sent Wyatt's blood pressure into the stratosphere.

Was she deliberately trying to torture him?

Dropping his arms to his sides, he said, "What kind of game are you playing, Lizzie?"

She didn't get up, but instead, looked over her shoulder at him. "Game?" One eyebrow lifted up in challenge. "What game?"

He took a step toward her. "You know what I'm talking about."

The corner of her mouth quirked up, then she slowly, provocatively, stood up straight. "I'm not quite sure we're done, Mr. Creed."

"I don't know what you mean, Ms. Martin." Like a magnet being drawn to its opposite pole, he drew closer to her. The whiff of her intoxicating scent nearly sent him to his knees.

She turned to smirk at him, then took the lollipop out of her mouth. "Usually, when you take a class or course, you're supposed to finish all the way through." Her gaze dropped low to his lips, then she touched the tip of the lollipop to his mouth.

He seized the stick from her hand, fighting the urge to lick the sticky residue of candy and Lizzie from his lips. "So, you came here because ..."

"I think I'm owed the rest of my lesson."

All blood left Wyatt's brain and surged straight down to his cock. That was the only way to explain his next words to her. "One more lesson then. Agreed?"

"Agreed."

"And which lesson would you like to learn?"

The tip of her tongue flicked out to lick at her lips. "The advanced one."

The lollipop dropped to the floor.

Jesus Fucking Christ.

"Tell me how to please you, Wyatt."

"It would please me to have you bent over this desk with your legs spread."

Her pupils blew up, and her arousal tinged the air.

"But first things first. Give me your panties."

"What?"

"Give them to me." With regret, he thought of the torn pair he'd tossed out this morning. "Now."

"Why?"

"Because I want them."

Reaching under her skirt, she bent down and slipped the panties off before handing them to him.

He pocketed the scrap of pink lace. "Thank you."

"You're welcome. Now what?"

Taking both her hands, he planted them on his chest.

"This part of the lesson is more self-study," he said. "Do what you feel like doing, and I'll tell you to stop or keep going."

"All right." Her fingers trembled as she unbuttoned his shirt, her eyes devouring him when she pushed the fabric away to reveal his chest. Standing on tiptoe, she pressed kisses along his pecs, her tongue darting out to flick at his nipple. When his body jerked, she stopped.

"N-no, keep going." It would kill him, but he decided it was worth it.

She wasted no time and slid her hands over his abs, then unbuckled his belt and unzipped his pants. Her mouth parted in a gasp when she ran her hands over his bulge. She gently squeezed it. When he didn't protest, she slid her hands into the waistband of his briefs to pull his cock out.

"Don't stop now," he teased, "or you won't get good marks."

"I'll have you know, I was a straight A student," she retorted as her fingers encircled him. "And I'm always willing to do extra credit." Slowly, she began to stroke him. "Is this okay?"

"Yes ... just a little tighter. That's it." He groaned when her thumb teased the bulbous tip. "There. Not too hard. *Argh!*"

"What?" She let go of him. "Did I hurt you?"

"No, no." He placed her hand around him again. "It just gets too much. That part is sensitive. But keep doing what you were doing."

"Aye, aye, captain," she said with a grin and tightened her grip. As her hand moved, Wyatt thrust his hips in time with her strokes, sending shivers of pleasure running up and down his spine. Grabbing the back of her head, he bent down to capture that luscious mouth of hers, savoring the delicious mix of sugar and Lizzie. His tongue matched his motions, stroking her and teasing her mouth in rhythm with his hips. When the knot at the base of his spine tightened, he reluctantly pulled away. "Ugh ... too much."

"I guess that's an A-plus?" she asked with a giggle.

"No need for extra credit," he groaned.

She tsked. "The thing with us prodigies is that we always do the extra credit." Getting down to her knees, her blue eyes widened as she faced his erection.

"Lizzie, you don't have to—oh damn. *Fuck*."

Her mouth was on his cock before he knew it. Seeing her luscious lips around the tip nearly gave him an aneurysm. She swirled her tongue around the underside, then pushed her head down to take more of him in.

Wrapping his hand around her ponytail, he began to guide her, showing her the speed he liked and encouraging her as she moved her mouth up and down his length. Lizzie was a quick study, of course, and she learned how fast he liked it and all the pressure points on his cock that made him moan.

"Stop," he said in a guttural tone as he gently pulled away. Helping her up, he guided her back to his desk. "Turn around."

She obeyed. "And?"

"You know what I want."

With a nod, she bent over the side of the desk, then spread her legs. "Is this good?"

"Perfect." Yes, that's what she was. Goddamn perfect in every way. Flipping her skirt up, he squeezed the plump flesh of her ass. "Hmmm, wet already." He swiped a finger across her swollen pussy lips, then brought it up to his lips. "Delicious." Wanting more, he kneeled down and licked at her.

"Wyatt!" she squealed, pushing back against him. "Oh ... yes, yes!"

He feasted on her was if he hadn't eaten in days, licking and sucking loudly at her sweet quim. She squirmed and grew wetter by the second. He slipped a finger under her to stroke her clit and soon, she was coming on his mouth, flooding it with more of her sweet juices. Fuck, he needed her now. Had it been less than twenty-four hours since he'd been in her? It felt like ages.

Standing up straight, he grabbed his cock and pointed it at her entrance. However, before he could push in, he remembered he wasn't wearing any protection. "Shit, I don't have a—"

"Condom?"

To his surprise, she already had one in her hand. Looking over her shoulder, she reached back to hand it to him with a grin.

The little minx planned it all along.

"Thank you."

"You're welcome."

As soon as he managed to get the rubber on, he thrust all the way into her. She let out a delighted cry as he filled her. He rocked into her, enjoying the feel of her pussy gripping him and the soft little pants she made. The tightness and feel of her were the only things he could think of as he continued to pummel into her.

Pulling her up so she was nearly vertical, he shoved a hand under her sweater. He tore at her bra and found her erect nipple. A soft pinch had her moaning loud, her pussy gripping him tighter. He rolled the nub between his fingers, which made her cry out and push back at him harder, her body shuddering as she tightened around him when she came.

He could do this all day, just have her impaled on his cock and making her come over and over again. Wring her dry until she gave him every ounce of pleasure she could.

"Wyatt!" she cried out.

He stopped, slid out of her, then quickly twisted her around to face him. Digging his fingers into her thighs, he pulled her back onto his cock, then closed his eyes and buried his face in her neck. As he continued to fuck her, he inhaled deep, committing her scent and this moment to memory. Sweat formed on his brow as he held back his own impeding orgasm.

Or perhaps he was just trying to delay the inventible. *One more lesson.* At the end of this session, she would leave again, and the time when she would be with Maxim drew ever so closer. A growl ripped from his chest, and he heard a howl from deep inside him.

"Please, oh, Wyatt," she begged, wrapping her legs around his waist, pulling him deeper.

The smell and feel of her was too much, and he would have had better luck pushing a waterfall upward than trying to stop his orgasm. With a guttural cry, he came hard, his cock pumping into her relentlessly as he wrung one last cry of pleasure from her. Her sweet body pressed against his, her spine going all rigid as she called out his name. He tightened his grip on her, pretty sure she would bruise, but he didn't care. He would leave his mark on her somehow.

Their breaths came in deep pants before synching to a

normal pace. Her arms loosened around him, but not before she pressed a kiss to his clavicle.

"Thank you." Her eyes were still glazed over as she looked up at him. "That was wonderful, Wyatt."

"You're welcome." He took a step back, removed the condom, then tossed it into the trash can before righting himself. "Did you, uh, want to get cleaned up? I have my own bathroom." He gestured to the door on the left.

"Hmmm, I think I'm good." She slid off the table and smoothed her skirt and sweater down. "I should probably get going. Your assistant said you had to run to another meeting, so I didn't want to take too much of your time."

In his imagination, he trapped her against the desk and asked—no, commanded—her to stay. *You're not going anywhere, Lizzie. I'll tell the entire office to take the rest of the day off while I fuck you on this desk until you beg me to stop, and even then, I won't be done with you.* Good God, he would gladly die tomorrow if he could just—

"Hey, what's this?"

Her question yanked him out of his fantasy. "What?"

She picked up a card on his desk. "This?"

"Ryan must have put it there." He squinted at the cream-colored card stock. "Looks like an invitation to a charity event. I get tons of those."

She flipped it over. "This one has the Silver Securities Tech Worldwide logo on it."

Irritation burst through him. "So?"

She read aloud, "'You are cordially invited to a charity ball to benefit the Code Girls Academy—'" She gasped. "Oh, I love that school, they're amazing!" She clutched the invitation to her chest. "They offer scholarships for underprivileged girls who want to get into tech. It looks like Silver Securities is the major sponsor. Maxim will probably be there."

A knife-like pain twisted in his gut. He'd been inside her less than a minute ago, and she was already saying another man's name. "I suppose."

"This is perfect! Can't you see?"

He didn't answer for fear of what would come out of his mouth.

She clucked her tongue. "This is it. Where we can stage our breakup. We can pretend to have a fight, break up, and then Maxim will see it." She looked at him expectantly, like waiting for him to agree.

The thought of handing Lizzie over to Maxim Silver after what they had shared sent a stabbing pain through his chest, like an axe cracking his ribs open. "I ... suppose it's a simple solution."

"Exactly. And it's tomorrow too, so we don't have to keep this up much longer. I'll be out of your hair in no time," she chuckled, then put the invite down on the table. "All right, we're all set then? I'll just meet you there at seven, if that's okay? We're super swamped at Lone Wolf, as you can probably guess."

"That's fine."

"Don't worry, I'll find something nice to wear. It's white tie, after all." She winked at him. "Okay, see you tomorrow. Thanks again."

Wyatt couldn't move, but only watched Lizzie as she gathered her things and bounded out the door. As he watched her leave, a revelation dawned on him. Of the three words he desperately wanted to tell her, but couldn't verbalize.

Wyatt would have laughed if it wasn't so fucking tragic.

There was only one choice if he wanted to preserve his sanity and what was left of himself. He had to let her go.

Chapter Ten

As soon as the elevator doors closed, Lizzie allowed that cheerful, nonchalant facade to melt away. *Elizabeth Eowyn Martin, you fool.*

She banged her forehead against the cool steel door. Whatever had possessed her to come here and seduce Wyatt?

It was just practice, she told herself when she decided to visit him. And if Wyatt said no, it wasn't like she would lose anything. They'd already had sex, and he promised he would respect her no matter what. She'd been nervous as hell, and the entire thing had been thrilling to say the least.

The ache between her thighs turned into a needy throb and her she-wolf whined with need. His scent, too, lingered on her skin like perfume. Despite not having anything to compare it to, she could definitely say that sex with Wyatt was fantastic.

But now she wasn't so sure if it was worth it. Since last night, she'd been trying not to wallow in a pit of loneliness and need, trying to claw her way out. She had to stop thinking about Wyatt.

She nearly succeeded too, but her impulsive side got the best of her, and now, she was in much deeper.

They had an agreement. No emotions. Yet, the strings she'd promised not to form were slowly wrapping themselves around her. That event tomorrow had been a gift and she was glad she thought of it. If she had to spend any more time with him, those strings would surely turn into a noose.

Maxim was the goal, she reminded herself.

But first, she had to break up with Wyatt.

Well, not really because they weren't together for real.

Ugh, why did I have to suggest we break up at that party?

For someone who was awkward around other people, she'd been going to a lot of parties lately. But if she wanted to end up with Maxim, she would have to get used to it, she supposed. An important man like him would expect his girlfriend to be his date at stuff like that. Besides, for once, she would actually be attending an event that was for a good cause, one that she personally supported.

Except she didn't have anything to wear.

Yikes. She didn't even know what white tie was exactly.

But she knew someone who did.

"Eames, I need to go to Hannah's please."

Right away. Your car is just around the corner.

Half an hour later, Lizzie found herself entering the Hannah Taylor Muccino Bridal boutique in SoHo. She breezed through the showroom and into the back where Hannah, her brother Anthony's wife, had her office and workshop.

"Hannah?" As usual, her sister-in-law was at her drafting board in the corner by the window, but she wasn't alone.

There was a tall figure next to her, looking over her shoulder. "Olivia?"

Her cousin, Olivia Jones, looked up from where she was standing next to Hannah. Her violet eyes widened with surprise. "Lizzie!" Graceful as a gazelle, she bounded over to Lizzie and embraced her. "I've missed you so much!"

"We message all the time on our group chat," Lizzie laughed, pushing away strands of fine silvery blonde hair from her face as they released each other from their fierce hug. Standing back, she looked up at Olivia—and she had to really stretch her neck back because her cousin was over six feet tall—and grinned at her. "But you're right, it's nice seeing you in the flesh, so to speak. Weren't you just in Paris?"

"Milan." Thanks to her height and stunning good looks, Olivia was one of the most sought-after supermodels in the world. "But I flew in because Hannah asked me to do her Spring show next year. I was actually on my way to Lone Wolf to see if you were around. Maybe you could help me get that brother of mine to take a break and have dinner?"

"Probably not." Arch, Olivia's older brother, was a terrible workaholic. "I'm glad you're here. You didn't happen to cross paths with Charley while you were zipping all over the world, have you?"

"Nah, I think she's in Seattle this week." Their other cousin, Charlene "Charley" Forrest worked as a production assistant for musicians on tour. "With—"

"The Douche Hole." Lizzie finished, gritting her teeth. Apparently, Charley's newest boss was terrible and mean to her, and thus was dubbed The Douche Hole—combination douche and asshole—because one insult wasn't enough to describe him. Lizzie had offered to get revenge on him for

Charley several times, but she said she would handle it herself.

"So, it's nice to see you and all." Olivia's silvery brows knitted together. "But what are you doing here at Hannah's?"

"I ... oh." *Oh crap*. Hannah she could trust to be discreet, but Olivia would want explanations. "Hey, Hannah, I was, uh, wondering if you could go shopping with me and help me find a dress?"

"A dress?" Hannah frowned. "For whom?"

"Uh, me. I sort of, uh, have to attend this thing tomorrow. "

Olivia leaned forward. "What *thing*? You're going to a *thing* that requires a dress?"

"Yup. It's a charity event for this girl's academy. See, it's this school...." She launched into a long explanation about the Code Girls Academy, extolling their program, and how they help more women into tech and coding. She also sprinkled in some technical terms here and there, most of them she made up. Her long-winded exaltation had its desired effect as both women's eyes had glazed over by the time she finished. "So, will you help me shop for a dress?"

"I think I might have something in the back, actually, if you wanted to borrow something instead," Hannah said. "A sample from my bridesmaid collection. Just about your size, and I can make any minor alterations if necessary. Stay here, I'll go grab it."

"Really? That would be awesome. You're the best, Hannah!" she called out as Hannah strode off in the direction of the storage room.

Olivia crossed her arms over her chest. "So, a charity event huh? This wouldn't happen to be a date, is it?"

If only the body was as cooperative as a computer, Lizzie could have stopped all the blood flowing up to her cheeks. "It's not what you think."

Taking Lizzie by the arm, she sniffed at her hair. "*That* is the unmistakable scent of male and sex. *Mmm,* fresh too. You were just with him, weren't you?" She blinked. "Lycan for sure. No one I recognize though. Who is it? Someone new from work? Another clan?"

Thank goodness she wasn't familiar with Wyatt's scent. But Lizzie didn't want to lie to Olivia. That and, well, her cousin was terrible at keeping secrets and if she told her, everyone in their family would know.

"Can I ask for a forty-eight-hour moratorium on that? I promise, I'll tell you everything." After tomorrow night, she and Wyatt would have "broken up," and maybe she'd have Maxim's full attention. *Hell, maybe I'll even be able to laugh about it.* The pit in her stomach, however, told her otherwise.

Olivia's mouth twisted. "All right. But I want all the details, okay?"

"Of course."

"Can I tell Charley at least?"

"*No,*" Lizzie hissed. "Forty-eight hours."

"Fine."

"Here it is." Hannah announced as she came back, a light blue bundle in her arms. "Go on and change over there."

Lizzie accepted the gown, headed behind the changing screen set up next to the wall, then proceeded to change out of her outfit and into the dress. "How do I look?" she asked as she stepped out from behind the partition.

Olivia gasped. "You look stunning."

"Really?"

Hannah dragged her over to the full-length mirror. "Really. Check it out."

"Oh. Hey," she greeted her reflection in the mirror. The dress was a light blue concoction made of tule with a sweetheart neckline and off the shoulder sleeves, showing off a modest amount of cleavage. She definitely looked *different*, but she wasn't sure if stunning was the right word, especially when she was next to the tall and willowy Olivia, who was a like a goddess even in her outfit of a simple white shirt, jeans, and black high heels.

"It matches your eyes perfectly," Hannah said.

"You're like a fairytale princess," Olivia added.

"Or an elf queen," Hannah quipped. "I knew it would look good on you. But it's missing something ..."

"Gloves," Olivia suggested. "It's white tie after all."

Hannah hurried off and came back with a matching set of elbow-length gloves which Lizzie put on. "Ah, there you go. Hair up or down?"

"Down." Olivia untied Lizzie's ponytail, letting it fall down her shoulders. "God, I'd kill to have your hair. Mine never holds a curl."

"Definitely down." Hannah agreed. "Perfect, looks like I don't even need to do any alterations."

"Thanks so much, Hannah, you're a doll." She hugged her. "I promise I'll give it back to you in one piece," she joked. "And I owe you a favor." She went back behind the screen and changed back into her street clothes. "I'll babysit Blaise for a week," she added as she took the garment bag Hannah offered her.

"Pleasure's all mine. And you know, just between us, I'd

been secretly hoping that you'd ask me to make you a dress someday."

Puzzled, she asked, "Really? Why?"

"Because you're gorgeous, dum-dum," Olivia said impatiently, then let out a sigh. She placed her hands on Lizzie's shoulders and stared down at her with a serious expression. "I just hope this date you're trying to impress is worth it."

"Date?" Hannah's tone pitched higher. "What *date?*"

"Olivia," Lizzie groaned.

The corner of Olivia's mouth quirked up. "Lizzie's got a hot date at this charity event. Someone she's also been—ahem —seeing for some afternoon delight."

"No. Really?" Hannah giggled. "Spill, Liz!"

Olivia and her big fat mouth! Lizzie groaned. "Look, I promise I'll explain everything." *Eames! Car, now!* "But later, okay? Toodles!"

Shifting the garment bag under one arm, she rushed out of the studio before either of the women could stop her. It seemed like forever before her car got there, and when it did, she quickly slipped into the backseat.

Whew.

Lizzie relaxed, feeling the adrenaline drain out of her. She just had to make it to tomorrow. Go to the charity ball, break up publicly with Wyatt, and then soon, she'd have everything she wanted.

I'm finally getting what I want.

Right now, she needed to concentrate on her future, and that future could only have Maxim Silver in it.

Seven on the dot, Lizzie arrived at the Waldorf Astoria Hotel. Alighting from her car, she smoothed her hand down her dress, glad it didn't wrinkle on the way here. As she entered through the doors, the mix of perfume, sweat, and various other smells hit her nostrils from the throng of people filling the lobby. But there was no sign of Wyatt.

She hoped he didn't change his mind or decide not to show up. She didn't dare contact him beforehand to remind him or even try to see him. But if he'd already forgotten about her then it wouldn't be so bad. At least that's what Lizzie tried to convince herself, despite the knot in her stomach and her she-wolf's protests.

Why did I even think of this public breakup? Surely, she could have found another way to let Maxim know she was available. Especially not one that involved having to see Wyatt again.

You can do this. Shaking her hands, she let out a deep breath to psych herself up. All she had to do get through the evening.

"Lizzie?"

The rough baritone sent heat straight to her core. Turning around, she faced Wyatt. "Uh, hi, Wy—" She had to take a gulp of air as the sight of Wyatt looking incredibly handsome in his formal tux walloped her in the gut. His coat was tailored to fit his broad shoulders and narrow waist, while the snowy white shirt and tie contrasted against the bronze skin of his neck. Her temperature shot up a few degrees as she recalled how that tan extended all the way down his body.

However, it was those light eyes that had her mesmerized. Eyes that stared at her in wonder.

"You look incredible," he breathed.

"I ... you too." She forced out a laugh. "See, I told you I wouldn't embarrass you."

"I never doubted you." He offered her his arm. "Shall we?"

Wordlessly, she took his arm and allowed him to lead her into the Grand Ballroom. She'd been here many times before as this was where the New York clan celebrated nearly all their events. Tonight, however, it was filled with unfamiliar people in glittering gowns and formal black tuxedos. Normally she would have felt out of place and awkward, but having Wyatt next to her was calming both to her and her wolf. She focused on the man next to her.

"Ah, there you are."

Lizzie stiffened at the sound of Maxim's voice.

"Silver," Wyatt greeted as they pivoted to face him.

"Don't you look lovely," Maxim said, his eyes fixed on Lizzie. "I'm so sorry we had to leave you back in Miami. I had an emergency at work."

"It's fine, everything worked out."

"I'm glad to see you accepted the invitation, Wyatt," he continued. "This academy means so much to me. I hope you'll consider getting more involved and possibly becoming a patron. We need more women in tech."

Wyatt stopped a passing waiter and took two glasses of champagne from his tray, handing one to Lizzie. "That we can agree on."

Maxim raised the flute already in his hand and grinned. "To women in tech."

"To women in tech," Wyatt replied.

Lizzie took a sip of the bubbly as an awkward silence passed between them.

"Lizzie, do you want to dance?" Maxim asked.

"Actually, I'd like to be her first tonight," Wyatt interjected, plucking the flute from her and handing it to Maxim. "Dance, I mean."

Lizzie's stomach did a somersault at his words. "I, um. Sure."

As he guided her to the dance floor, Lizzie's heart thudded in her chest like a drum. "I don't know how to dance," she confessed when they reached the middle.

His hand slid down from her back to her waist, his fingers gripping her, then leaned down close to her ear. "I'll teach you," he said, his warm breath caressing her skin as he pulled her close so their bodies touched and her face was right up against his chest.

A blend of nerves and excitement swirled in her belly as his other hand caught hers and they began to sway with the music.

"Just follow along."

"Th-this isn't so bad." Despite her own warring emotions, something about this, being so close to him, smelling him, feeling the warmth of his body and hearing the thudding of his heartbeat ... felt so right. "You're a good dancer." Warmth enveloped her, wrapping her in a blanket of comfort and ease.

"My grandmother insisted I learn." He twirled her around, then brought her back into the circle of his arms. "What will you say to him?"

"Say to who?"

"To Maxim. Why we're breaking up tonight."

His words slammed into her, and that comfortable feeling

dissipated. "Um, I guess I could just tell him we decided we're too incompatible."

"Incompatible," he repeated flatly.

"I mean, c'mon, look at us. What a joke, right?" She attempted to sound lighthearted, hoping to lift the heavy cloud that hung around them like an ominous presence.

"Right. We're too different."

"Uh-huh." She nodded vigorously. "You're like, a billion-aire CEO playboy, and I'm just a tech geek."

He bit his lip as if he wanted to say something then changed his mind. "I like old-fashioned things like reading books, and you probably wouldn't survive a whole afternoon without your phone."

"Try a whole hour," she grinned. "You'd bore me to death talking about Proust and Aristotle."

"And my eyes would start glazing over the moment you waxed lyrical about the latest processor on the market."

"I'd hate going to parties like this all the time."

"And I'd hate staying indoors, staring at screens all day."

While the couples around them continued to dance and the music played on, they had stopped swaying at some point and were now standing still, eyes fixed on each other.

"Well then, I guess this is where we say goodbye." He nodded behind her. "He's looking this way."

She glanced over her shoulder where Maxim was, indeed, staring at them intently. "I guess so."

The fingers on her waist flexed, gripping tighter. Her throat tightened, the words she wanted to stay were stuck there, so she begged him silently.

Don't let go.

"Goodbye, Lizzie. I wish you all the best." And with that, he released her, turning his back to her as he walked away.

Tears gathered in her eyes, but she willed them not to spill. Her entire body felt numb, and inside her, her wolf paced around, confused.

"Lizzie?"

She inhaled deeply and rubbed her eyes with the back of her hand. "I ... Maxim?"

"What's wrong?" Gripping her arms, he turned her to face him. "Did something happen? Did he say something to make you cry?"

She stiffened. "It's not—"

He tipped her chin up so she had to look into his face. Dark blue eyes searched her. "What did he say?"

Not knowing what to tell him, she spoke the truth. "That we're just too incompatible." Her chest ached as she said the words. "It's not working out."

"Oh, Lizzie, I'm sorry. I knew something was up last weekend and then he just left you." He tsked and put his arm around her, pulling her close to his chest. "It's all right, don't worry."

The smell of his aftershave made her nose wrinkle in distaste, and she gently pushed away from him. "It's all right. These things happen." She sniffled and tried to smile, but failed.

"Don't worry, Liz. I'll take care of you."

Wrapping his arm around her shoulder, he ushered her away from the dance floor, guiding her through the crush of people. Her vision blurred as, to her horror, more tears spilled down her cheeks.

Why am I crying? This was stupid. She knew the plan all

along. Fake relationship, no emotions, no strings. Yet, Wyatt's hold on her would not loosen.

I can't do this. There had to be a way to just stop feeling like this.

"Lizzie?"

Glancing around she found herself outside the ballroom, right by the elevators. "Th-thank you." Away from the cloying crowd, she could breathe better, though her chest was still trapped in a vice-like grip.

"I'm so sorry, Lizzie. I can't believe he just left you like that." His jaw set hard. "Bastard. Didn't even want to do it in private. Probably didn't want you to make a fuss. I've heard things about him you know, about how ruthless and calculating he can be."

"He's not," she denied. "Not like that, I mean. Not with me." No, Wyatt was anything but cold to her.

"You're still in shock. You probably didn't expect to get dumped in the middle of a dance floor." He clucked his tongue. "Do you want to get cleaned up and composed? Maybe have a drink to calm yourself? I have a suite upstairs. We could, I mean, *you* could have some privacy." A hand went down to the small of her back, squeezing her there lightly. "But I could come with you too ... if you want."

Lizzie did not miss the meaning in his words. *This is what I wanted, right? Maxim Silver is the man I want.* She'd gotten this far. All she had to do was take the next step.

The elevator's soft ding announcing its arrival jerked her out of her thoughts.

"Lizzie?" Maxim held the door open. "Are you coming?"

"I ..." She took a deep breath. "Yes."

Chapter Eleven

Wyatt was going to be sick. Honest-to-goodness, vomiting up the dinner he barely ate from earlier in the evening, *sick*.

Either that or he was going to destroy *something*.

Though he left Lizzie on the dance floor, he remained at the party, staying a good distance from her. And sure enough, he wasn't even gone five minutes when that bastard swooped in. He watched, barely able to contain his rage as Maxim guided her away and led her to the elevators, his entire body turning numb as she walked in right behind him. Unable to bear it, he made his way outside, pushing past the doors and stumbling out into the cool evening.

"What the fuck? Watch it, moron!" came the indignant shout from the angry New Yorker he'd crashed into.

Wyatt snarled at the man, who jumped back.

"Holy shit! Your eyes!" The look of abject terror from the man satiated Wyatt for a moment. "Crazy motherfuckers," the man cursed as he scampered away.

Good riddance.

There was a gasp behind him, and he turned around to see a group of elderly matrons staring at him, pure shock on their faces.

But he didn't care. One singular thought was on his mind.

Lizzie was going to fuck another man.

Right now, she was probably getting naked. Kissing Maxim, letting him kiss her in all the places Wyatt had kissed and licked and tasted first. Maxim would get between her legs and—

The growl that ripped from his throat was inhuman, but Wyatt didn't care.

He was going to kill that rival male and claim Lizzie for himself.

Pure rage ripped through him as he raced back into the hotel, not caring that he was using his superhuman speed in public to make it to the elevators in a split second. He jabbed the call button repeatedly, willing the damned thing to come faster.

When he heard the soft *ding*, he let out a breath. "Finally." The doors slid open and he took a step inside, shoulder forward and ready to knock back anyone who dared get in his way. Clouded by the red-hot fury raging through him, he failed to see the other passenger coming out. When the scent of strawberries and champagne hit his nostrils, he staggered back, as if the globe had stopped spinning under his feet.

"Lizzie?"

Soft hands gripped his arms, preventing him from falling back. "W-Wyatt?"

He blinked away the red haze surrounding his vision

until an angel clad in ice blue tulle appeared before him. "You're here." He could not hide the ache in his voice, nor the relief when he added, "You didn't go with him."

"I ... almost did, but I came back down before we reached his suite." She inhaled a quick breath. "Wh-what are you doing? I th-thought you'd left."

"I couldn't. I had to come back." His throat clenched tight.

"Why?"

"I had to stop you from sleeping with him." His hands came up to grip the sides of her face. "Because, Goddammit, I'm in love with you." Saying the words aloud, hearing them come from his own lips was terrifying, but at the same time, freeing. "I'm so fucking tired of pretending I'm not, of preparing you to be with someone else when it should be *me*. Me who you should be with and want to do all those things with. Going on dates, snuggling on the couch on rainy days. Weekend getaways, brunch on Sundays, family events." His heart raced harder than it had ever done, even harder than when he was fighting for his life against the mages. "I love you, Lizzie. Only you, from the very beginning. And I will love you until the end."

"Wyatt." Her hands cupped his chin. "I want to do all those things with you. No one else. I love you too." She gasped and blinked. "I shouldn't ... Oh go—"

He cut her off with a kiss before she could take the words back. No way in *hell,* not even if Satan himself came crawling out of the ground to force her, would he let her take them back. Lizzie *loved* him. If his heart gave out right this moment, he would die a happy man.

Something from deep within urged him to claim her, mark her as theirs so no other male would dare take her away from him. Keeping his grip on her, he walked her back into the elevator and smashed his fist into the row of buttons. Somehow, he hit the correct one and the doors *swooshed* into place.

"Wyatt," she groaned as his lips trailed down her neck. "Shouldn't we ... I mean, let's go back to your—"

"No," he growled against her skin. "Now. Need you now."

"What? Oh! One sec." She laid her palm against the panel, then the elevator went dark. "There you go—oh!"

Wyatt pulled her skirt up and ripped her panties, splitting them down the middle. He was already rock hard, his erection jutting painfully as he unzipped his pants. Bending down, he lifted her up, pushed her against the wall and impaled her on his cock. She was already soaking wet, so he slid right in.

"Wyatt!" she moaned as her arms came around his neck.

"Fuck, Lizzie ... so good." He gasped as she gripped him tight, the feeling of her raw so different from the other times he'd been inside her. There was something pure and primal about having no barriers between them. "Perfect. You're perfect. I love you."

"I ... love you too." She cried out as he began to thrust into her.

He buried his face in her neck, breathing in her scent, losing his mind in the smell and feel of her. It was all too much, and he wouldn't be able to last long, but he didn't care. All he wanted to do was claim her. Erase any trace of another man from her.

Lizzie let out a whine when he stopped. "Wyatt?"

"Did he touch you? Kiss you?"

"No, it never went that far."

"Good." He claimed her mouth in a bruising kiss. "I'll kill any man that touches you."

She shuddered, letting him know she understood how serious that threat was. Pinning her against the wall, he reached up to rub his wrists along her neck, marking her with his scent so they would know she belonged to him.

"You're mine, Lizzie." He gave her lips a nip. "From now on, I'm the only one that gets to touch you and fuck this pretty little pussy of yours, understand?"

He felt her nod and heard her whimper of pleasure, her pussy pulsing around him. "You need me, don't you? Need me to fuck you good, my Lizzie?"

"Y-yes."

"Need me to come inside you?" he whispered. "Fill you up with my cum?"

"Please. Yes. Wyatt." She gripped him good again. "Come inside me."

He let out another primal roar and began to pummel into her. Hard and fast. Everything around him blurred except for Lizzie, the feel, smell, taste, and sound of her. When her body shook with her orgasm, he let go. His cock pulsed several times filling her with his hot cum, and in the darkened elevator, stars burst in his vision as the most intense orgasm on his life battered his body. The force of his pleasure engulfed his entire body—his entire being—until all he could think of was Lizzie. He slowed down, finally stopping when the feeling returned to his lower body.

"Wyatt," she sobbed against his chest.

With a deep sigh, he withdrew from her, gently placing her back down on her feet and righting her skirts back into place. He pressed his sweaty forehead against the cool metal wall, waiting for his heartbeat to return to normal.

Lizzie pressed her face against his chest. "Did you really mean it? What you said?"

He pushed away from the wall to face her, his enhanced sight adjusting to the dim light so he could look at her face. "How could you doubt me after that? I love you, Lizzie." He frowned. "You love me too, right? You didn't say it just because I did?"

"What? No?" She hopped up to give him a quick kiss on the lips. "I didn't want to break up with you. I mean it wasn't real. Not at the beginning. But after we ... after that first time and you said you didn't want any emotions involved, I was already stupidly falling for you. I came to your office yesterday because I wanted more."

He smiled. "I'm glad you did. I didn't want to break up with you either. And to me, it felt real. I didn't want it to be just pretend. I meant what I said, I've wanted you from the beginning. Since I saw you again."

"You did? Why didn't you say anything?"

"It didn't seem appropriate, considering the important work we were doing." He shrugged. "End of the world and all that."

"Right. Whew." She pursed her lips and blew out a breath. "I'm glad you came back for me tonight. Thank you."

"Are you always going to thank me after we have sex?" he teased.

"It's practically a tradition now, isn't it?" She straightened his bowtie, then touched the wall panel, bringing the elevator back to life. "*Now*, can we go back to your place?" She had the biggest smirk on her face.

"With pleasure."

So, Wyatt took her to his apartment and made love to her in every way, and six, seven, *and* eight ways to Sunday.

And Lizzie thanked him each time.

Chapter Twelve

"Oh wow," Lizzie gasped.

"Yeah, wow." Wyatt echoed.

She kissed his naked shoulder. "Not that I'm complaining or anything, but really? *Here?*" She glanced around at blinking lights from the stacks of servers around them. Currently, her bare ass was pressed against Row G, Rack 2, which managed all the print jobs in the Creed Security building. The prickly server had protested when Wyatt had pushed her up against it, so she had no choice but to shut it down. Hopefully no one was waiting for an important document.

"I thought you liked computers?" He lowered her feet back down on the floor, then tugged her skirt back down.

"I talk to computers," she reminded him. "I don't necessarily like all of them. Do you like all the people you talk to?"

"No." He cupped her chin and kissed her. "But I love you."

A thrill shot up her spine as it always did when he told her that. "I love you too."

It had been three days since the night of the ball, and Wyatt and Lizzie had spent every moment they could together outside work, from evening until dawn, wrapped up in each other's arms in his penthouse. The sex was amazing each time, but Lizzie liked cuddling with Wyatt afterwards, just talking about nothing. Well, she talked about nothing and he just lay there and listened, playing with her hair and nibbling at her skin.

She hated leaving him each morning, but they both had lives so reluctantly they parted each time. This morning, though, the servers at Creed alerted her to an anomaly, so she raced over there. She figured she'd check out what was wrong first, then go up to see Wyatt to convince him to play hooky the rest of the day.

Well, that had been the plan anyway. She had just finished checking on the security systems when Wyatt had come in, all alpha male and horny, and started tearing at her clothes before she could protest.

"You could have waited," she said. "I had planned to head up to your office as soon as I was done."

"Why didn't you come to me first?" His voice turned low and rough. "I had to hear from my IT manager that you were here." There was an edge to his voice. "I would have come with you."

"What for?" She pulled her bra back into place, then righted her T-shirt, soothing her palms over the cute koala print on the front. "I think I know my way around a server room."

"That's not the point. I don't want you alone here with all those IT geeks drooling all over you." His nostrils flared. "I told you what I'd do if any other man touched you."

Lizzie bit her lip. On one hand, this jealous side of Wyatt brought a thrill all the way to her bones. But on the other, murder was still illegal. "Baby," she soothed, placing her hands on his chest. "I only want you, remember?"

He gritted his teeth and then reached over to rub his wrists on her neck. Leaning forward, he inhaled at the skin below her ear. "Hmmm ... I love your scent, especially when it's mixed with mine. Don't try to rub it away, I'll know if you do."

Well, I guess I'm not going back to the office today. Every single Lycan at Lone Wolf would know right away she'd been with Wyatt.

He got down on one knee, then made her step into her panties, which had been dangling from one ankle. Pulling them up slowly, he stared up at her.

"I guess I get to keep my panties this time," she said with a smirk. He already had a nice collection of her underwear at home, refusing to give them back to her each time she stayed over.

Ignoring her statement, he fixed the panties back into place. "Don't try to wash me away, either. I want you walking around with my cum dripping from your pussy."

As if on cue, her clit throbbed at his dirty talk. Fuck, this man was turning her into some kind of sex fiend. *I'll make him pay, somehow.* "So, no playing hooky, huh?" She pouted.

"Afraid not." He slipped his arms into his shirt and began to button it up. "I have this important meeting—one that I'm already late to."

"And whose fault is that?"

He chuckled as he zipped up his pants. "Entirely mine,

and I don't regret it." He kissed her again. "I have a surprise for you tonight."

"A surprise? I love surprises! What is it?"

His eyes slid heavenwards. "Woman, don't you know what surprise means?"

She blew out a breath, sending a red curl flying off her forehead. "Fine, fine. Your place, I assume?"

"Seven. Sharp. Don't be late." His hand snaked around her waist to pull her in for a possessive kiss. "And don't let any of those IT guys near you."

She sighed against his lips. "Aye, aye, captain."

Lizzie let him leave first, if only to make sure no one ran into them together. After giving the servers one last check, she packed up her things and left the room. "Eames, tell Dad I'm stuck in traffic and that I'm working from a cafe the rest of the day."

Will do.

Leaving the Creed Security building, Lizzie decided against taking a car and instead, began to stroll uptown towards Broadway. Her thighs and knees still ached, so she took her time.

What could Wyatt's surprise be?

She was pretty sure sex would be involved but after three nights of their non-stop dusk-till-dawn sex marathons, she wasn't sure if there was anything else he could possibly surprise her with. It seemed they'd already boinked in every position possible and every surface of his place. Heck, he'd even asked her to bring some of her favorite toys, which had been ... interesting to say the least.

Her stomach grumbled. *Ugh, again?* She's scarfed down two burgers and large fries before she went to Creed, and that was after she's had a whole plate of fried rice and walnut shrimp from Emerald Dragon for lunch. But then again, sex did burn a lot of calories, especially the athletic, energetic kind she had with Wyatt.

Sighing, she stopped at a cafe and ordered three bagels and a coffee. As she sat down to eat, an idea popped into her mind. One way she would pay him back and tease him. She would show up at his place tonight—wearing only sexy lingerie.

Elizabeth Eowyn Martin, you slutty, genius whore!

She nearly choked on her coffee as she chuckled to herself.

After finishing her food and throwing her trash away, she caught a car to an expensive department store in Chelsea. She had no idea how to buy lingerie, but there was a first time for everything. She supposed she could ask Olivia if she was still in town, but surprisingly, she hadn't heard from her cousin, considering the forty-eight hours she had asked for had expired. She didn't even realize as she'd been so caught up with Wyatt. *Olivia probably had to jet off to London or Shanghai.*

She strode into the lingerie department and picked up a few items—stockings, and a matching bra and panty set in white that had strings of pearls for straps. The panties looked incredibly uncomfortable but she wouldn't be wearing them for a long time anyway.

After paying, she took a car back to her place, put on her new lingerie, and covered it up with a trench coat. By the time she walked into the lobby of Wyatt's building, it was already ten minutes past seven. Hopefully Wyatt wouldn't be too mad that she was late. She giggled to herself. *Wyatt won't even notice once he sees what I'm wearing.*

Waving at the concierge, she strode right into the elevators and pressed button for Wyatt's penthouse. *Ugh.* The pearl panties were much more uncomfortable than she'd expected. She adjusted the straps, then straightened herself once the elevator slowed down.

Wyatt Creed, get ready to have your world rocked.

The doors opened, revealing Wyatt, arms crossed over his chest, a stern look on his face. "You're late."

"Sorry," she said in her most seductive voice. "I promise I'll make it up to you." Untying the belt of her coat, she shrugged it off, letting it fall to the ground. "Like it?"

Wyatt's hazel eyes grew as big as dinner plates. "Lizzie, you should—"

Lizzie jumped on him before he could finish, her legs wrapping around his waist as she pressed her mouth to his. Caught by surprise, he staggered back, knocking into the console table by the door. She tightened her grip around him, but didn't release his lips, though for some reason, he was intent on pushing her away. "Wyatt, what's the matter—"

"Wyatt? Did I hear something break—oh my!"

Lizzie froze at the sound of the familiar feminine voice. She caught his gaze. "Wyatt?"

He sighed. "We're fine, Mom," he called out.

Mortification flooded Lizzie, and she prayed for the earth to swallow her up. Turning her head toward the living room, her stomach dropped as she saw Jade Creed standing there, frozen to the spot. Her husband, who entered right at that moment from the dining room, rushed to her side. "Jade, are you—what the fuck?"

Lizzie had never seen the dragon shifter looking so completely and utterly shocked. "Uh, hi, Mrs. Creed." She swallowed a gulp. "Mr. Creed." Untangling her legs from Wyatt, she got back down to her feet. He shielded her body from them, not that it would have done any good as his parents had already seen plenty. "What the hell is this? Your parents?"

"They were the surprise," he said. "Well, one of them."

"There's *more?*" she asked, incredulous. "Who else did you invite? The mayor? The entire Tri-State area?"

"I, uh—" The soft ding of the elevator announced the arrival of more guests.

"... are you sure this is the right place?"

"That's what his text message said."

Lizzie groaned aloud. "Oh no. Please, no!"

Selena and Quinn Martin stepped out of the elevator. "See?" Lizzie's father said. "I told you this was the place—oh, and here's—" He stopped short as his gaze landed on Lizzie. "What the hell? Lizzie?"

"Oh fuck." Lizzie slapped a hand to her forehead. "This is a complete and utter nightmare."

"Lizzie?" Selena's mouth opened into a perfect O, probably because she saw what her daughter was *not* wearing as she tried to hide behind Wyatt. "Why are you here?"

"I think it's obvious." Quinn Martin's face twisted into a mask of fury, his skin turning the color of a tomato. Lizzie could practically see the steam coming out of his ears. "What the fuck is going on here, Creed?"

Wyatt moved to speak, but was interrupted by his mother as she strode over to Lizzie's parents. "Quinn, Selena, how lovely to see you again." Jade Creed was the picture of grace and calm. "Sebastian and I were mixing some drinks in the dining room. Care to join us?"

"Not until this fucker explains himself." Quinn looked ready to take Wyatt's head off. "You ask me and my wife to come to dinner? What for? To show me how you're fucking my daughter?"

"Quinn!" Selena hissed.

"That's two dollars in the swear jar!" Lizzie joked, then shrank back quickly when her mother looked daggers at her.

"Sir," Wyatt began, his voice as calm and composed as his mother. "I love your daughter, and she loves me."

"What?" Selena's face slackened and Quinn's jaw nearly dropped to the floor.

"I invited you—and my parents here—to let you know that Lizzie and I are together now."

"You did? Why didn't you just say so?" Lizzie groaned. "Why did you tell me you had a surprise?"

"Oh, I don't know, because I wanted to surprise you?" he replied casually. "We would have had to tell them eventually, so I thought I'd make it easier and have them both over at the same time."

"Ah. Right." She patted his shoulder. "Good plan."

"Except for the part you decided to show up in lingerie and a trench coat."

"Uh, yeah, sorry about that," she said sheepishly. "But I can't believe ... you really wanted to tell your parents? And mine?"

"Lizzie, I want to tell the entire world."

Her heart melted, and she embraced him. "Wyatt, I ..."

"Ahem."

They froze as Sebastian Creed strode over to them, stopping only to bend down to pick up Lizzie's coat. He then handed it to Wyatt, who wrapped it around Lizzie. "How about that drink, Quinn? Selena?"

"Sounds like a great idea." Selena hooked her arm through her husband's. "Come on, Quinn, let's ... leave the lovebirds to compose themselves." She hurriedly dragged her husband away from Lizzie and Wyatt, trailing behind Jade and Sebastian.

Lizzie buried her face in Wyatt's chest, which started to rumble with laughter. "It's not funny."

"Oh, it was pretty funny." Tipping her chin up to face him, he smiled at her. "Thank you for the surprise. I do love it."

"You're welcome." She reached down to adjust the panties. "But I don't know how I'm going to sit through dinner—with our parents—with a string of pearls riding up my ass."

He flashed her a naughty grin. "How about I promise to make it worth your while afterwards?"

"Deal."

Seeing as she couldn't have dinner with just the lingerie and trench coat on, Lizzie borrowed a pair of boxers and a shirt from Wyatt, then joined everyone in the dining room. To her relief, the two couples were laughing and chatting when they entered.

"Oh, Lizzie," Mrs. Creed waved her over. "I'm so happy for you both."

"It really is sweet of Wyatt to invite us here, right, Quinn?" She elbowed her husband.

Quinn—whose face had returned to a normal shade—turned to Wyatt. "I think next time, I'd prefer an email."

"He's joking," his wife added. "Though there's no need to be so formal, really."

"My son's always been formal and proper," Sebastian added with a raise of his whiskey glass. "He does things the right way."

Lizzie thought she imagined it, but she could have sworn Wyatt flinched. Frowning, she gripped his hand. "Most of the time."

"How did this start?" Selena asked. "You never even told me you were dating, and now you're in love?"

"It's long and complicated," Wyatt said. "But I've known Lizzie was the one for me for a while now. I just didn't want to risk anything because we were working so closely at the Guardian Initiative."

"He must have known since Lake Hope," Jade suggested. "He risked his life trying to save her."

"Or before that, when he snuck into the Fenrir basement facility to beat the crap out of that bastard who hurt Lizzie," Sebastian added in a smug tone.

"That bas—wait, what?" Lizzie looked up at him, puzzled. "Jean-Baptiste?"

Wyatt's grip on her hand tightened. "I couldn't let him get away with hurting you."

Sebastian tipped his chin up at his son. "Damn right." A look passed between father and son, and Lizzie observed Wyatt visibly relax.

"So," Wyatt began. "As I've already told Mom and Dad, I

invited an up-and-coming chef to make us dinner tonight. He and his staff will be serving us." He nodded to the young man who was standing by the doorway that led into Wyatt's massive kitchen. "Please tell Mr. Jacobo that we're ready to begin."

"Yes, Mr. Creed," the young man replied, then turned on his heel and disappeared into the other room.

"Fancy," Lizzie said with a whistle. "You're pulling out all the stops, aren't you?"

He grinned at her. "I aim to impress."

"Here you go, your favorite," Selena said as she handed Lizzie a glass. "Dirty vodka martini, extra dirty—"

"And extra olives," Lizzie finished with glee. "Thanks, Mom!" Holding the glass to her lips, she took a sip—then promptly spit it out. "Eww, I think there's something wrong with those olives. *Blech.*"

Her mother frowned and took a sip from the glass. "Tastes fine to me. I—" Her eyes widened briefly, then she looked over to Jade, who had a similar expression on her face.

"Well—" Lizzie was interrupted by the sound of the elevator chime. "Oh, did you invite anyone else?"

Wyatt's eyebrows knit together. "No, just the six of us."

"Hey, bro! You having a party without me?" Bastian said as he strode into the room.

"Bastian?" Wyatt looked bewildered. "What are you doing here?"

"Bastian messaged me that he was flying back tonight," Jade explained. "And since you invited us to dinner, I thought it was a family thing and told him to stop by if he arrived in time."

"Yeah, looks like I came just in time too! Who's—" His

mouth snapped shut when his gaze landed on Lizzie and her parents. His head snapped toward Wyatt, then back to Lizzie again. "What—holy shit!" His hands covered his mouth. "Holy shit, bro! You really did it, didn't you? You motherfucker!" Slapping Wyatt on the shoulder, he let out a laugh. "I knew it wouldn't take you too long to get your head out of your ass and admit that you were one hundred percent *gone* for Lizzie."

Wyatt snorted but said nothing.

"What?" Lizzie asked incredulously. "You knew too?" She glanced at Wyatt's parents. "All of you?"

"Apparently, everyone around you did except the two of you," Selena chuckled.

"Am I that stupid?" she groaned.

Bastian ruffled her hair affectionately. "Nah, just dense as to how much of a catch you are." When Wyatt sent him a warning look, he took a step back. "I'm glad for you both. And I hope you guys are happy."

"We are." Wyatt snaked his arm around her shoulder.

"So, can I stay for dinner?"

"Of course you can, son," Sebastian answered. "Right, Wyatt? Surely your fancy-schmancy chef can whip up an extra meal for your brother?"

The arm around Lizzie dropped. "I ... of course, let me talk to him. Excuse me."

"I'll come with—" But Wyatt was already gone.

A tight knot grew in Lizzie's stomach. Something was going on with Wyatt, but she didn't know what to make of it. He'd been in high spirits most of the night, especially after declaring his love for her in front of their parents. Now she could sense the anxiety growing in him, could even feel the tension stretching him thin, but what had changed?

A boisterous laugh had her head snapping over to Sebastian and his younger son, who looked as thick as thieves while they conversed animatedly. From the way they interacted, it was as if there was no one else around. The pride on the elder Creed's face was evident as he listened to his son regale him with tales of his latest business deals and adventures.

"They're going to set up an extra seat," Wyatt announced as he re-entered the dining room. "If you don't mind waiting a minute."

"Not at all," Bastian said. "Thanks, bro."

When Wyatt came back to her side, Lizzie reached up to touch his cheek. "Everything okay?"

Turning his head, he kissed the inside of her palm. "Of course, why wouldn't it be?"

"Are you—"

"C'mon, let's sit down."

Lizzie followed Wyatt, unsure what else to say. *Maybe I'm reading too much into this whole thing.*

For the rest of the evening, Lizzie convinced herself that everything was fine. The dinner was actually a fun affair, with everyone contributing to the conversation. Well, almost everyone. Wyatt remained silent beside her, only responding if anyone asked him a question directly. There was still tension radiating from him, but it was as if only Lizzie could sense it. She also noticed that he became even more tense whenever Bastian spoke.

Lizzie bit her lip. Wyatt had never mentioned any bad blood between him and Bastian. In fact, from what she gathered, they were close. What was going on?

After they finished their dessert and the plates had been cleared away, Chef Jacobo came out to greet them, and they all praised him for his food before he and his crew packed up and left.

"Well, that was a fun dinner," Bastian declared. "Now how about we all head over to Blood Moon for an after-party?" Blood Moon was a Lycan bar in Midtown. "It'll be fun," he said. "Just like old times."

"Oh no, my partying days are over," Quinn said.

"Mine, too, son," Sebastian added. "But I'm so glad you were able to make it to dinner."

"We need to invite your sister next time," Jade added. "Whenever she can get away."

"Oh, how is Her Highness?" Selena asked. Wyatt's sister had married the king of a small kingdom some time ago and was now his queen consort.

"She's doing great." Jade turned to Wyatt. "Give her a call and tell her your news?"

"Of course, Mom," he replied. "I'll do it first thing in the morning."

"I guess you and Lizzie aren't coming to Blood Moon then?" Bastian asked.

"No thanks," Lizzie said. "I've heard it's terrible now with all the tourists." Blood Moon was supposed to be a safe space for Lycans, a place where they didn't have to worry about being discovered. It even had magical protections around it. Lizzie wasn't so sure how that magic worked, but apparently it made it so humans would ignore its presence or become uncomfortable being there. However, ever since the Lycans were outed, it seemed not even magic could keep the curious humans away and now they came in droves, perhaps hoping to see the Lycans turn into their wolf forms.

"Staying in, gotcha." He winked at Wyatt. "Well from the look on your face, bro, I think it's time to leave you love-birds alone."

"We should be going anyway," Selena said with a yawn. "It's way past our bedtime. Thank you so much for inviting us, Wyatt." She embraced her daughter. "Give me a call, soon, okay? We need to *talk*."

Lizzie cringed inwardly. She recognized that tone of voice from her mother. The one she used when she was dead serious. "I will."

"My daughter is perfectly capable to taking care of herself, I made sure of that," Quinn said to Wyatt. "So, if you do her wrong, you should know that even *I* won't be able to find your body."

"Understood perfectly," Wyatt said in a polite tone.

"Good." Still, Quinn offered his hand, which Wyatt shook. Then he engulfed Lizzie in a bear hug. "Holler if you need anything."

"I will." She lowered her voice. "You're happy for me, right?"

"As long as you are." He kissed her temple. "I'll see you at work tomorrow."

Both Jade and Sebastian hugged her too as they said their goodbyes, and promised they would all get together again soon, as the two moms were already planning a joint Thanksgiving celebration.

Finally, all the lingering goodbyes were said and their guests piled into the elevator. As soon as the doors closed, Lizzie turned to Wyatt. "Are you sure everything's—hey!"

Wyatt picked her up with no effort, and slung her over his shoulder, fireman style.

"What are you doing?" she shrieked, which he replied to with a firm slap on her ass. "*Yeow!* That hurt!"

"I think you enjoyed it." He nuzzled at her hip. "You're getting wet already."

Ugh, she hated it when he was right. "Wyatt, please can you put me down for a sec? Can we talk?" She'd been waiting to be alone the whole night so she could ask him what was wrong. Because something definitely was up with him. She needed to know what was wrong and fix it for him.

"Talk later," he grunted, then gave her ass another slap. "Sex now."

Lizzie went all limp. "Fine."

Maybe she had just been imagining that something was wrong. She and Wyatt were happy and in love, and that was all that mattered.

Chapter Thirteen

Last night's successful dinner—and her and Wyatt's private "after-party" proceeding after it—should have made Lizzie content and more than satisfied. She had what she wanted—a boyfriend who loved her and could experience all the normal couple things with.

Yet there was something still not right.

Elizabeth Eowyn Martin, can you be content?

But there was something about last night and Wyatt that bothered her. Sure, when they were alone, he'd been just as attentive and eager as he'd been since they first slept together. But she couldn't help but feel there was something off.

Her she-wolf yowled, trying to get her attention.

Do you feel it too?

It answered with an affirmative nod.

But what did it sense?

The loud knock from outside her door startled Lizzie, and she nearly jumped out of her chair. She'd been staring at the same screen for the last half hour, ever since she came back from lunch, trying to finish her report and analysis on the cyberattacks on Creed, as well as the steps she planned to take to secure the networks. It reminded her that there were other things going on outside her personal life. Finding the culprit and stopping them was high priority right now.

"Come in!" To her surprise, Maxim Silver's tall, elegant form emerged from the doorway. "Oh—hey, Maxim."

"Hello, Lizzie." Maxim closed the door behind him. "I just finished meeting with your uncle, and so I thought I'd check on you. So ... how have you been?"

"I'm doing great, thanks."

"Are you sure?" He crossed his arms over his chest and leaned back on the door. "You didn't seem fine when you left me at the charity ball."

"Oh, uh, well ..." She searched for what to say, then settled on the truth. "I'm sorry I just ran away without an explanation. But it wasn't a good idea to be alone with you, Maxim. I was emotional and not in the right state of mind."

"Because Wyatt broke up with you?"

"We had a misunderstanding," she corrected. "One that we cleared up right away. There's no need to be concerned about me. Wyatt and I are perfectly happy together, and in fact, we had dinner with our families last night to tell them about us."

He let out an exaggerated sigh. "It's true what they say then, the good ones are always taken."

"You'll find someone someday, Maxim."

"Not like you."

Had he said that to her a week ago, it might have brought a thrill to her.

"Lizzie, are you—whoa!" He stumbled forward as if

pushed by in invisible force, crashing into Lizzie's desk as the door flew open.

"What the hell are you doing here?" Wyatt burst in, all fury and fire, hands curled into fists at his sides. His glare could have burned flesh and bone. "You stay away from her!" He lunged for Maxim.

"No! Wyatt!" Lizzie jumped over her desk and pulled him away. "Stop. Don't do this."

"What is he doing here alone with you? With the door closed?" Wyatt roared.

"He's a client," Lizzie hissed.

"I just stopped by to check on her." Though his tone was even, Maxim was visibly shaken. "I didn't get a chance to see her home after the charity ball. After all, her date left her standing alone in the middle of the dance floor."

Wyatt's face twisted in rage. "Why you—"

Lizzie put herself between him and Maxim, but shot the latter a dirty look. "I told you, we made up. It's all fine."

"Everything okay here?"

All three of them froze, then turned toward the doorway. Arch Jones stood there, calm as a millpond, but Lizzie could feel the dominant vibes of his wolf radiating from him. He was the spitting image of his father—except for the violet eyes he shared with his younger sister—and just as commanding. Lizzie had heard from her father that back in the day when they were Lone Wolves, Uncle Killian had been their leader, and perhaps if he'd had his own territory, would likely have ruled as Alpha. It was obvious his son was just as dominant, if not more.

"Everything's fine," Lizzie said with a gulp. Her she-wolf cowed in submission.

"What is he doing in here?" Wyatt demanded. "Why is he allowed to just roam the offices like he owns it? With all the sensitive information around here, you should know better, Arch."

Arch glanced briefly at Lizzie before speaking. "I know you're a client now, Mr. Silver, but Wyatt is correct. That doesn't give you a right to just barge into anyone's office. We take the privacy of all our clients seriously. I'm sure you can appreciate that."

"Of course. You're the one who brought me in as a client, after all," he reminded him. "I just wanted to see Lizzie. Can't I say hi to a friend?"

"She is not your friend," Wyatt roared. "She isn't anything to you."

"Let me escort you out, Mr. Silver," Arch offered diplomatically. "I can show you which parts of our office are open to clients so you don't get lost next time."

"Of course. Forgive me for overstepping my bounds." He gave Lizzie a nod. "I'll see you around."

Before Wyatt could say anything, she grasped his arm. "Bye, Maxim."

As Arch led Maxim out, he shot a Lizzie one last glance, to which she replied with a grateful smile. The news of her relationship with Wyatt had reached the family group chat earlier that morning, which she had expected. She already had a ton of messages from Olivia and Charley, who wanted all the details.

"You are never to be alone with that man," Wyatt seethed. "If he even breathes on you, I'm going to kill him."

"Oh, for fuck's sake, Wyatt, it's not even three o'clock, and you're already threatening murder." Lizzie had to admit it had been hot the first few times, but now it was alarming. "Nothing happened, he just wanted to say hello."

Wyatt's arms remained stiff at his sides, his hands balled into fists. "I don't give a fuck what he wants."

She placed a soothing hand over his chest. "C'mon, baby, calm down. I'm yours, remember? I love you and no one else."

That seemed to mollify him as he caught her hand, then kissed her wrist before rubbing it on his neck. "Your scent drives me crazy."

Before she knew it, she was flat on her back on top of her desk, with Wyatt nudging her knees apart. "What—oh God, no!"

He paused. "No?"

She pointed to the corner of the room. "We have cameras all over the place."

"Oh." Clearing his throat, he pulled her upright. "I ... sorry." A hand scrubbed down his face. "I don't know what got into me. Something was blocking your office door and I thought the worst ... and sure enough that asshole was in here. What did he say to you? Did he hit on you?"

"He'd only been here a minute when you burst in." She shrugged. "Like he said, he was just checking in. That night, I just kind of, er, ran away from him without any explanation, and I haven't seen him since. I'm sure he was concerned." Gingerly, she touched his arm. "Wyatt, what's the matter? Can you talk to me, please? You've been acting weird since last night."

For moment, something shifted in his expression, but a cool mask quickly replaced it. "Nothing's the matter." Hands gripped her waist as he pressed his nose to her hair. "Especially now that I'm with you. My Lizzie." His body relaxed against her. "You're all I need."

Her she-wolf scratched at her, as if willing her to listen, but Wyatt's scent and body distracted her. "Hmmm ... I really wish I could turn off those cameras."

"Can't you?" he murmured against her temple. "Just for five minutes."

"Five minutes? That's not enough time," she said with a giggle. "Besides, I can't. Company policy." Pulling away, she looked up at him. "By the way, what are you doing here so early? You said you'd pick me up after work tonight."

"Yeah, about that ... I couldn't wait." He flashed her a naughty smile. "I regret not playing hooky with you yesterday, so I thought I'd remedy that. I told Killian I needed you to check on something at Creed. Might be an all-day job too."

"And all night." Her hand wrapped around his tie and tugged him down. "Where should we go? My place is closer. Or how about a room at the Hilton down the street?"

He gave her a quick peck on the lips. "Come with me and find out?"

"Oh yeah."

As it turned out, Wyatt's idea of playing hooky extended much farther than a room at the Hilton or the Lower East Side.

"Where in the world are we?" Lizzie asked Wyatt as his private jet began its descent.

"Vermont."

"Vermont?" she repeated. "Like, the state of Vermont?"

"Yes. I have a house here. I thought it would be perfect for a first weekend getaway."

"Weekend—oh!" Not caring about safety, she unbuckled her seatbelt and jumped on his lap to pepper his face with kisses. "This is amazing,"

When they landed, there was already a black Range Rover waiting for them on the tarmac. Wyatt drove them out from the airstrip and further up the mountains, where all the leaves had already turned red and golden, painting the landscape in the brilliant colors of fall.

"This isn't a house," Lizzie declared as they stopped outside the enormous stone and log structure at the end of a long private driveway. "It's a mansion. How much land do you have here?"

"Fifty acres," he declared, cutting off the engine. "And I don't have neighbors for miles. We're all alone here. The staff prepared everything we need until Sunday."

The inside of the mansion was even more beautiful. Everything was wood and stone except for an entire wall with huge glass windows that had a magnificent view of the mountains. The fireplace lit the sunken living room in a romantic glow.

"Do you like it?"

"I love it!" She jumped into his arms. "And I love you."

Wyatt walked them over to the fireplace and lay her down on the plush sectional couch. "I love you too, Lizzie."

They made love slowly, but eagerly in front of the roaring fire, and Lizzie forgot about the outside world for just that moment. In here, with Wyatt, miles and miles away from everything, all she could think, breathe, and feel was him. He held her so tight as their bodies joined, she feared her body would break, but she knew he would never hurt her.

"Oh God, that was amazing ..." she sighed as she collapsed on top of his chest. His cock softened inside her, so she rolled onto her back. "I think my soul just left my body." Smiling, she turned to him. He was staring straight up, his eyes glazed. "I'm not the only one."

"Lizzie?"

"Yes?"

"Marry me."

"W-what did you say?"

He shifted onto his side to face her. "Marry me."

"What?" A chuckle burst out of her. "I mean, the sex was amazing, but not enough to warrant a proposal."

His expression did not change. If anything, his pensive stare intensified. "I mean it. Be my wife."

He was *serious*.

Breathe, Lizzie, breathe.

"Are you sure? I mean, we've only been officially together for less than a week. Maybe you shouldn't make such a rash decision and you should think—Wyatt?" Her heart sank as he rolled off the couch. *Oh no, I've made him angry.* "Wyatt." She sat up. "Please, can we talk about this?"

He walked over to his discarded pants on the floor and picked them up, though he didn't put them on. Instead, he fished something out of the pocket, then strode back to her. Opening up his palm, he revealed a shiny object.

"Wyatt?" Her jaw dropped. "Is that—"

"I bought this ring the day after you told me you loved me too." He got down on one knee and held the enormous sparkling diamond between his fingers. "It's true we've only been official this week, but I've been waiting for you for almost two years—no, my whole life. I don't need to think this through. So please, Lizzie, don't make me wait any longer. All those things you want—the house in the suburbs, the two-point-five children, the dog—I want them too. With you. I love you."

Tears sprung in her eyes. "I ... yes, of course, I'll marry you."

Wyatt's face lit up in the biggest smile she'd ever seen on him. "I love you, Lizzie." He slipped the ring on her finger. Rising, he wrapped his arms around her and pulled her in for a fierce kiss. "You've made me so happy."

"Me too." She grasped the sides of his face to look deep in his eyes. In that moment, her she-wolf scratched at her, once again trying to point out something to her.

But what?

"How about some dinner?"

Her stomach answered with a growl. "Yes, please."

Wyatt laughed. "I told my staff to stock up triple what they usually do when I come here by myself, since you seem to have a healthy appetite."

"Well, I have been more active than usual," she said with a wink.

He grinned. "Let's go get something to eat before you starve to death."

"Uh-oh, are you sure you want to marry me? I might eat you out of house and home with my voracious appetite."

"It's *our* house now," he said. "And you can eat to your heart's content. I'll give you everything you want and more. You're all I need in the world."

There was something about the way he said those words

that made her throat close up. The statement should have elated her, but there was a hollow sadness to it. She desperately wanted to ask him again what was wrong, but it didn't seem like the right moment. They were happy and engaged; he was giving her everything she wanted. She could not ruin this beautiful moment, and so she swallowed her questions along with her doubts. "All right, let's go eat, I'm starving."

Chapter Fourteen

It was Sunday morning, the last day of their weekend getaway, when Lizzie woke up to the most peculiar sensation. Her ears twitched and her nose wrinkled, and there was a scratching coming from deep within her, followed by a woeful yowl.

Oh.

Her she-wolf wanted out.

How long had it been since she'd shifted?

For Lycans like her who lived in the city, there was not a lot of chances to shift into their wolf forms. There were strict rules about when and where they could change. But generally, it was a good idea for Lycans to let their wolves out, not just to release their pent-up tension, but also for practice. When Lycan pups came of age and started to shift, they all went to a kind of bootcamp training where they learned how to control and work with their wolves so as to prevent accidental shifts that could cause harm and reveal their secret to the world.

Lizzie did her training at her Uncle Jackson's ranch in the

Shenandoah Valley in West Virginia, and she and everyone in the family went there regularly to visit and let their wolf sides out. After the craziness during the mage attack, she and her brother Jacob had gone there to lay low. At the Shenandoah clan's ranch, they could roam about in their wolf forms without worry.

Glancing over at Wyatt, she nudged him with her shoulder. "Wyatt?"

He murmured something in his sleep, but didn't wake.

Her wolf grew impatient, so she had no choice. Slipping the diamond ring from her finger, she placed it on the side table before slinking out of Wyatt's enormous king-sized bed.

She didn't bother getting dressed as she padded out of the master bedroom and down the stairs. As soon as she was out the door, her wolf ripped out of her. The enormous strawberry blonde wolf dashed straight into the woods, flying across the dirt, her paws barely touching the ground.

Had she forgotten how freeing it felt to just be in her wolf form? How her senses were even sharper, and she could see, hear, and smell *everything*—from the robin sitting high up on the tree, to the rustling of a rabbit from a mile away, and even the pungent scent of pine sap hanging in the air.

Maybe once she and Wyatt were married, they could come here every weekend to spend time in the woods. It would be the perfect place to teach their pups how to shift and play and live in harmony with their wolf sides.

The wolf's ears perked up at the sound of a familiar voice calling out, and without Lizzie's intervention, she steered their shared body back toward the house. Sure enough, Wyatt was there on the enormous back porch, calling out her name. She picked up her pace, leaping up over the flight of stairs to land a few feet from Wyatt. Stalking over to him, she encircled him and rubbed her furry flank across his legs before shifting back.

"Good morning," she greeted, slipping an arm around him from behind.

"Where were you?" His voice was tight and body stiff.

"My wolf just needed to run. It's all the space and mountain air and greenery." She brushed her cheek against his back. "Hmmm, come for a run with us. I want to see your wolf again."

His body tensed even more. "No, thank you." Twisting around to face her, he caught her hand and slipped her engagement ring back onto her finger, the gold surprisingly cool on her skin. "Don't ever take this off."

"I didn't want to destroy it when I shifted," she said with a chuckle. "You know that." She frowned when he remained impassive. "Wyatt? What's wrong?"

His hands dropped to his sides. "Nothing. It's fine. I was just scared when you weren't in bed and I saw the ring. I thought ..." He bit his lip.

"You thought what? That I left in the middle of the night? You're being silly, Wyatt. Now, c'mon and shift with me."

"I ... don't want to."

"Don't want to?" She gestured around them. "All this land, with no one else in sight, and you don't want to shift? Your wolf must be dying to get out." She grabbed at the bottom of his shirt. "Wyatt?"

He brushed her hands away. "I just don't feel like it, okay? Can we just drop it?"

"I—" Her mouth clamped shut. He'd never been short

with her. Not like that. "I … okay, if you don't want to, I won't force you." Her throat tightened.

"Lizzie …" He reached out to touch her shoulder. "I'm sorry, I didn't mean … I thought something happened to you. I don't like not waking up next to you."

She stepped into his arms. "Nothing's going to happen to me."

"You're moving in with me tomorrow," he declared, tightening his grip on her.

"But—"

"We're already engaged," he reminded her. "Besides, you waste so much time in traffic going back and forth from my place to yours. If you want, we can start house shopping next weekend. We can live on Long Island, or—"

"Wyatt, slow down." She forced out a chuckle. "Why are you in such a hurry?"

"I just want to start our life together, Lizzie. Our own family. I thought you wanted that too?"

"Yes, but we don't have to do everything right now." Looking up at him, she sent him a reassuring smile. "I'm not going anywhere, okay? Understand?"

He paused, but nodded.

"Let's put a pin on this house discussion for now." She pressed a kiss to his chest. "I'm hungry. Can we please have some breakfast?"

"Of course, whatever you want. How about Sunday brunch? There's a small town about half an hour from here, and the cafe there serves the best pancakes with maple syrup in the country."

"Sounds great."

Lizzie leaned her head on his shoulder as they walked

back into the house, her hand rubbing soothing circles on his back. Some of the tension seeped out of him, but that underlying strain remained, swimming just beneath the surface.

How she wished she had more experience with relationships, at least the emotional parts. That way, she could figure out how to talk to him. Dread filled her at the thought of bringing up something that might burst their happy little bubble. But then again, she feared that if she stayed silent, it might all blow up anyway.

They returned to New York later that evening, and soon they were driving back into the city. As she sat in the back of the limo beside Wyatt, Lizzie glanced down at her hand, the engagement ring a heavy weight on her finger. Though the rest of their day played out like normal, she couldn't help but feel like something had fundamentally changed between them.

"Do you want to go out to dinner?"

Her head snapped up. "Huh?"

"We're here." Sure enough, the limo was stopped outside his building. "We can head to this French restaurant around the corner." He threaded his fingers through hers. "We haven't had a proper date night."

"Aww, you're too sweet. But can we just stay in tonight?" She gestured down at her yellow shirt that had a drawing of an alpaca wearing a hat, black leather skirt, and combat boots, which were the same clothes she had worn since Friday. "Besides, I don't think those snooty waiters will let me in there wearing this."

"All right. But this is why you need to move in with me right away," he stated firmly. "Why don't we go shopping for some new clothes for you? That way you don't have to bother with packing up your old ones, and you can start living with me tonight."

"I don't need new clothes." But Wyatt was already out on the sidewalk, holding the door open for her.

They walked inside, and Lizzie waved to the doorman and concierge as they crossed the lobby. As soon as they were in the elevator, Wyatt's hand slipped under her skirt, fingers inching up her inner thigh.

"Wyatt ..."

"We're all alone," he said, nuzzling at her neck. "Even if we weren't, then I wouldn't care. When we eventually have our date night, I'll slip my fingers into you under the table and make you come in a room full of strangers."

"Ohhh ..." Turning her head toward him, she nipped at his mouth. "Naughty."

"Uh-hmm." The elevator slowed to a halt and the doors opened. "Now, let's—"

"So, you're finally home."

Lizzie froze when she heard the unfamiliar female voice. Beside her, Wyatt quickly withdrew his hand from under her skirt and straightened up. "Grandmama? What are you doing here?"

Grandmama?

On the other side of the elevator doors was perhaps one of the most elegant women Lizzie had ever seen. She was dressed in a dark blue dress, pointy heels, and a mink stole draped across her shoulders. Though she was about Lizzie's height, her ramrod straight spine made her appear taller. It was difficult to guess her age, because although her artfully arranged hair was pure silver, there were very few wrinkles on her face. Of course, that could have been because her expression remained stony and unmoving. Her vivid blue eyes were currently trained on Lizzie like a hawk's.

"I've come for a visit. You gave me your key and said I could come anytime." Her accent was crisp and clean, like undisturbed fallen snow, and just as cold. "Though, really, you should hire a proper butler to open your door. Who is your guest?"

"Grandmama, this is Lizzie." Wyatt ushered her out of the elevator. "Lizzie, this is my grandmother, Fiona, the Lady Oxley. Grandmama, this is Lizzie Martin ... my fiancée."

"How do you do?" Lizzie held out her hand.

Lady Oxley did not shake her hand. Instead, those hawk-like eyes continued to scrutinize her, moving from head to toe before settling on the ring on her finger. "Fiancée? Since when?" Her nose wrinkled, like she'd smelled something rancid.

"He proposed this weekend," Lizzie informed her.

"I see." Her expression remained impassive.

"Grandmama, why don't you sit down, and I'll make us some tea?" He led both women toward the living room, directing them to the sofa. "You and Lizzie can get to know each other."

There was no way in hell this was going to end well for her, but before Lizzie could protest, Wyatt disappeared into the kitchen. Pasting on the most congenial smile she could muster, she gestured to the seat next to her. "Lady Oxley, do you want to sit d—"

The click of her heels on the marble floor cut Lizzie off as she moved away to the opposite side of the coffee table. She then perched on the edge of the armchair, her body turned out toward the window and away from Lizzie.

Taking her own seat, Lizzie observed Wyatt's grandmother. It was difficult to believe the warm and affable Jade Creed was even related to this woman. There was some physical resemblance for sure, but the cold, hard face revealed no emotion. And while perhaps there were some cultural differences between the English and Americans, Lizzie was pretty sure she was being ignored.

The silence between them stretched on for what felt like an eternity until finally, Wyatt came out of the kitchen with a tray.

"How was your flight?" Wyatt asked as he placed the tray on the table, then began to pour the tea into delicate white cups.

"Dreadful," she replied. "The food was terrible, as was the service. And of course, it only went downhill the moment we landed in JFK." Her pert nose wrinkled. "This city has not improved in the decades since I lived here."

"I'm terribly sorry, Grandmama." He twisted a lemon slice into a cup before handing it to her. "You should have told me you wanted to come for a visit, I would have sent the jet."

"Or you could have come back to visit me in England." She took a delicate sip. "Ah, this is from our tea shop on Bond Street, isn't it?"

"Of course, Grandmama."

"A touch of home and civility." The cup barely made a sound as she placed it back on the saucer. "I was hoping to speak to you. Alone."

Wyatt sat back down beside Lizzie and took her hand into his. "You can say whatever you want in front of Lizzie, Grandmama. She's going to be my wife."

"Indeed." She didn't even glance toward Lizzie. "It's been so long since you last called or paid me a visit. Aren't you coming back to England?"

"Grandmama, I told you, my life is here in New York. I'm the CEO of Creed Security now."

She gave a delicate harrumph, but said nothing more.

"Anyway, I'm glad you came, if a bit surprised." He put an arm around Lizzie. "You'll come back for the wedding, won't you?"

"Why not get married in England? It's so beautiful there. Maybe in the countryside, like in Hampshire or Surrey."

"New York can be beautiful too," Lizzie piped in.

That earned her an eyebrow lift. "I'm sure."

Lizzie looked to Wyatt. "Our families are here, of course we're having our wedding in America. It doesn't have to be New York. My uncle's ranch in West Virginia might be a good alternative."

"West Virginia?" Lady Oxley's nose twitched once more.

"We can talk about this later," Wyatt said. "Right, Lizzie?"

She shot him an incredulous glance. Did he try to deflect instead of agreeing with her? "If you'll excuse me, I need to use the bathroom." Rising to her feet, she strode off in the direction of the master bedroom.

When they spoke of his grandmother, Wyatt had made her sound like a kind, gentle woman who had taken him in when he found himself alone in a new place. Now, Lizzie wondered if there was more to it than that.

A pit grew in her stomach as her instincts told her, once again, there was something *not* right, not to mention, she could sense something off about Lady Oxley, but couldn't put her finger on it. It wasn't just because she ignored her; Lizzie was used to snobby people brushing her off. But there was something deeper that made her feel uncomfortable around the older woman.

Lizzie paced, twiddling her fingers and biting her lip. Deciding she'd been gone long enough, she headed back outside. She was nearly out the bedroom door when the voices drifting in made her pause.

"... and who is she? Who are her parents?"

Lizzie's heart stopped. She knew exactly who the *she* Wyatt's grandmother was referring to.

"Does it matter, Grandmama? She's part of the clan, and so are they."

"She's a Lycan?" She let out an indignant sound. "I cannot believe you've chosen this ... this clan over me once again. I'm your flesh and blood. You never should have come back here."

"You know why I came back, Grandmama. The mages were out to kill us and take over the world. How could I stand back and do nothing?"

"Oh, pishposh, you're being dramatic. We didn't know for sure at the time there was a major threat."

Lizzie covered her mouth. Did she really gloss over the fact that the mages were plotting to eradicate Lycans and essentially place humanity under their control?

"You should have let someone else handle it," she continued.

"Mom is part of this clan too," he reminded her.

"Ah, yes, your dear mother." She harrumphed. "What wasted potential. I should have insisted she remain in England."

"Then she wouldn't have met my father, and we wouldn't be having this conversation. Grandmama, can we please not get into this now? Lizzie is here, I want you to get to know her better."

"What happened with Sandra Collingsworth? I thought for sure the two of you hit it off."

Sandra Collingsworth? Lizzie ground her teeth together.

"We just didn't suit, Grandmama."

"I was so disappointed she told me that you didn't ask her on a second date. Her grandfather is Earl Granwith!" She tsked. "You went out with her last week, and now you're engaged to this ... this nobody?"

Wyatt went out on a date with a woman last week? Lizzie's anxiety turned into rage, and her she-wolf let out a snarl. *This bitch!* Stomping out into the living room, she roared, "Who did you go on a date with last week?"

"Lizzie, I can explain." Wyatt was calm as he stood up from the couch. "This was before you and I got together. We went to the ballet, then I dropped her off at her hotel. That's all. It was the same night I saw you at Bastian's."

She was mollified somewhat, but her wrath did not dissipate. So she turned to Lady Oxley. "Ma'am, I appreciate all you did for Wyatt growing up. But you have no idea how much we needed him back here. The mages were planning to kill us all and put humanity under their control. Wyatt saved me and three other people, plus, his work at the Guardian Initiate was crucial to the success of our mission. If he didn't come back, none of us would be standing here."

"Lizzie," Wyatt began. "You don't have to—"

"But I do," she said firmly. "She needs to know that the mage threat was serious. Your grandson was a hero, don't you care about that? Aren't you proud of what he's done?"

She turned to Wyatt. "You're going to let this insolent girl speak to me this way?"

Lizzie could no longer contain her fury. "Lady, what the hell is your damage?" Her animal came to the surface, ready to fight the other she-wolf. She faced the older woman, hands curled like claws, readying herself for ...

Nothing.

Lizzie gasped. There was no animal she or her wolf could sense from the older woman. It was as if Lady Oxley was completely human, which was impossible because Jade Creed was a full Lycan and there had been no True Mate pairing before their generation. "What's wrong with you?" she exclaimed, horrified. "What's wrong with your wolf?"

"Unlike you savages, I have learned to control that beast." Fierce pride dripped from her posh tone. "I've not shifted nor even felt that animal in nearly fifty years."

"But that's ... unnatural."

"I've managed quite well, thank you. I've built a life away from Lycans. I'm happy." Her eyes turned into slits. "At least I was until your idiotic Alpha revealed our existence to the world. You have no idea how this has upended my life. I've barely left the house in months. It's been like having a sword over my head that at any moment, one of my friends or acquaintances might discover my true nature. If word gets out, it would destroy me and everything I've worked for." Her nostrils flared. "I'm just glad my husband is no longer around or he would have figured it out."

"*That* was what you were worried about? That your fancy friends would turn their backs on you if they found out you were a Lycan?" *This selfish bitch!* "Didn't you hear what I said about the genocide of our kind and the destruction of life as we know it?"

"Wyatt, I'm tired of this conversation," she declared. "Tell this woman to leave."

"No need." She put her hands in the air. "I'll show myself out."

"Lizzie, please." Wyatt attempted to catch her arm, but she evaded him, striding quickly to the elevator. Before she could even reach for the call button, Wyatt was there, blocking her way. "Lizzie, you don't have to go."

"I know that. I *shouldn't* have to be the one to leave," she hissed. "But I can't listen to her bullshit any longer." *And having you stand there and say nothing.* Because the truth was that hurt even more—that he would allow his grandmother to disparage and disrespect their work and their Lycan nature.

"She's my grandmother," he stated.

"And I'm going to be your wife. I want to share my life with you, but I'm not going to stand around and stay quiet when she insults us and what we've accomplished. What she's saying ... it's so twisted and warped to deny what we are." Her own animal seethed inside her. "How could she do that to her she-wolf?" She wanted to weep for the poor creature.

"It's her choice," he shrugged. "Besides, what if she's right? What if we're the unnatural ones?"

Her jaw nearly unhinged. "Are you serious? Did you hear what you just said?" Gripping his arms, she stared up at him. "How could you say that? You—" The bottom of her stomach gave out, because when she attempted to reach out to his wolf, she could barely feel it.

That was what her wolf was trying to tell her all this time. Wyatt, too, had been locking his inner animal away.

She took a step back. "That's why you didn't want to shift with me."

"Lizzie, the threat of the mages is over. We're safe. You're safe. I won't let anything happen to you." When he reached for her, she shrank away.

"No! Don't touch me."

The color drained from his face. "Please, Lizzie. You're the only thing I need in this world."

"That's the problem, isn't it? I can't be everything to you."

"But I love you."

"And I love you. But you also have to learn to love yourself, for who and what you are. Please, Wyatt, don't let that ... woman tell you you're not good enough."

His jaw hardened. "She was the only one who ever thought I was good enough growing up. I wasn't ever second best to her. She was the only one who really loved me."

Her heart broke at his words. Clearly, there was something else going on. "I don't know what that"—she pointed toward the living room—"is, but that wasn't love back there. If she really loved you, then she would have accepted your Lycan nature instead of trying to suppress it." Wrangling her anger, she paused for a moment and weighed her options. She knew what she had to do. "I'm sorry, Wyatt. For whatever you've been through. I think ...I think we need to step back and think about this for a bit."

"What are you saying?" Desperation strained his voice. "Lizzie?"

Twisting the ring off her finger, she placed it in his palm. "I can't marry you." *Not yet*, a small voice inside her said. "You need to figure yourself out first. Who you are and which world you want to live in." She reached behind her to call the elevator. "Goodbye, Wyatt." She took a step back as soon as the doors opened.

He didn't attempt to stop her. Instead, his gaze remained fixed on the ring in his palm.

Once the doors closed, Lizzie buried her face in her hands and wept. Doubt crept into her mind, telling her to go back to him. Her instincts—hell, her wolf—had been screaming at her that something was wrong with Wyatt. And though she didn't know exactly what happened, the puzzle pieces began to form in her mind.

He'd been acting strange ever since that dinner with their parents, or rather, when Bastian arrived unexpectedly. Sebastian Creed spent most of the evening talking to his younger son, which was understandable because Bastian was always jetting off all over the world. But Lizzie wondered if that had always been the case since childhood. And perhaps, that vile woman somehow took advantage of Wyatt's loneliness and insecurities to twist him into her own image and make him hate what he was.

When the elevator reached the ground floor, she quickly dried her tears with her shirt, then proceeded outside as if nothing had happened. The crisp air slammed into her, soothing her, but the ache in her chest only grew.

I need to think.

Heading in the direction of downtown, she forced her legs to walk in an attempt to put as much distance between her and Wyatt. But the ache only spread further. She was halfway down the block when she stopped in her tracks.

I shouldn't have walked out on him. I should have fought for him.

What he needed was her love and understanding. For her to be his support when he was down. Wasn't that what real couples did for each other? It wasn't all Sunday brunches and weekend getaways and the big house in the suburbs. It was sticking together, not just through the good but also the bad. Helping each other instead of walking out when times got tough.

She spun on her heel, ready to march back when she bumped into someone who'd been behind her. "What the— Maxim?" A strong grip on her arm stopped her from toppling back.

"Whoa, careful there." He set her back upright, but didn't release her.

"Uh, thanks." She chewed at her lip. She'd been so caught up in her thoughts, she didn't hear him approach. Where did he come from?

"Lizzie, what a pleasant surprise running into you unexpectedly," he greeted, his voice unnaturally cheerful. "What are you doing all the way uptown?"

Glancing at the curb, she spied the Mercedes with the driver's door open. Did he stop and get out just to say hi to her? He'd left the engine running, too.

"I ... I was heading home. From Wyatt's." She wasn't sure why, but her wolf's hackles rose. "What about you? Do you live around here?"

"Just visiting a friend in the neighborhood."

Lizzie could smell the nervous energy around him. The

palm wrapped around her arm was unusually sweaty, especially considering the cool weather. And what was his other hand fiddling with in his pocket? "Are you all right?"

The smile on his lips didn't reach his eyes. "Why wouldn't I be?" He withdrew the hand in his pocket.

"What are you—ouch!" Her hand slapped at her neck as something pricked her. "Maxim?"

He tossed something—a syringe—to the ground. "I'm sorry, Lizzie." Reaching for her wrists, he ripped her smartwatch off. "Can't have you calling for help." His hand darted into her pocket, then tossed her phone aside.

"Calling for ..." A wave of dizziness passed over her, and her limbs loosened. "What ..."

"You're coming with me, Lizzie," he said in a menacing tone. "I need you."

"Need ... me?"

"Uh-huh. I know about your special powers." An arm slipped around her waist just as she lost feeling below her knees. "I just need you to do one job for me. That's all. Then I'll let you go. Just do it, and I won't hurt you."

Oh God.

She was being kidnapped!

Her she-wolf snarled and tried to rip out of her, but it let out a whimper.

Then the world went black.

Chapter Fifteen

Wyatt had never felt so bare and raw in his entire life until that moment when Lizzie's arctic blue eyes bore into his very soul and saw what he'd been trying to hide from her.

His wolf was broken. And it was all his fault.

All these years of trying to suppress his Lycan side, he'd finally succeeded. Sure, it surfaced briefly when he thought Lizzie was about to sleep with Maxim. But after that, when he finally thought he'd won Lizzie, he kept it locked down. There was no need for his Lycan side, not anymore. He had all he needed and wanted in the world—Lizzie.

But now he'd lost her too.

"Good riddance." Fiona's heels clicked across the marble floor as she walked up to him. "Wyatt, what were you thinking? That girl is entirely unsuitable for you. You must find a nice, human girl to marry."

Wyatt's hand curled around the ring in his palm. "A nice human girl? You mean, so I can have human children."

"Exactly." Turning him around to face her, she caressed

the side of his face. "Your human children won't have to suffer the indignity of having feral, beastly natures. They can live a normal life."

Normal life.

Yes, that's all his grandmother ever wanted.

Just to be normal.

"Wyatt, why don't you give Sandra a call—"

A growl ripped from his throat. "Stop it!" He pushed her hand away. "Lizzie was right." As he stared into her eyes, he finally recognized what he failed—or refused—to see all these years. Lizzie had seen it, though—the emptiness, the hollow shell that his grandmother had become. "Grandmama, I'm a Lycan. We're Lycans. We can't ignore that or pretend otherwise."

"But you can!" she insisted, grinding her heel into the floor. "There are ways. I succeeded after years of hard work, and I almost had your mother's wolf locked away too."

"Mom?" His stomach twisted and bile rose in his throat. "What do you mean? And how did you never shift for fifty years? What about Blood Moon?"

"I have my doctor put me under anesthesia every time there's a Blood Moon," she stated. "Your mother, too, when she was with me. After a few years, her wolf all but disappeared."

"You drugged her? That's child abuse!"

"You don't know what it was like, you insolent boy!" Finally, Fiona's well-controlled facade slipped. "What happened to her. When she was only eleven years old, she shifted on the way home from school. The wolf caused a panic, and her school bus flipped over. Children were seriously hurt. One of them suffered lifelong damage, and your mother nearly died."

His poor mother. "What did you do?"

"What I had to. To protect her and others. I took her away to England, away from this ... this savage life. But that ungrateful child undid all my hard work, no thanks to your father and their True Mate pairing."

His dad? *The True Mate pairing*. Finding her mate must have freed his mother's wolf.

"Can't you see, Wyatt? You don't have to live like this, constantly battling with that feral beast inside you. Come back to England with me. Forget about that woman, you don't need her. You can have normal children, not monsters."

The rage that had been bubbling inside him finally burst. "You're the monster, Fiona," he declared. "I should have listened to Lizzie." *Lizzie*. He needed to go to her, explain. Ask for forgiveness.

"Wyatt, what are you saying?" Her lips twisted into a snarl. "If you choose that little tart over me, I'll never speak to you again."

"Then perhaps you should go," he said in the most icy tone he could muster. "Goodbye, Fiona."

Shock registered on her face. "Wyatt, you can't be serious."

"I am deadly serious." He crossed his arms over his chest. "I'm going after Lizzie." The elevator would take too long, so he strode off in the direction of the staircase. "You better be gone by the time I come back or I'll get security to remove you."

"This is out—"

The staircase doors slamming behind him cut off his

grandmother's outraged protest. Wyatt's heart pounded in his chest as he took the steps two at a time. *Please don't let me be too late.* Once he reached the ground floor, he practically flew out of the building and into the street.

"Lizzie!" Taking a deep breath, he sniffed out the faint scent of strawberries and champagne. Following the trail, he swung his head in the direction of downtown—then froze as he saw Maxim Silver carrying an obviously passed out Lizzie toward a waiting car.

A vicious roar ripped from his throat as his wolf tore out of his human body. The massive brown wolf leapt forward, soaring in the air before landing on top of the Mercedes's hood, the metal bending under its weight.

"Fuck!" Maxim dropped Lizzie on the sidewalk, then sprang across the street. He barely made it halfway as the wolf chased after him, sinking its teeth into his arm to drag him back toward the sidewalk.

"Please, no!" he pleaded as Wyatt's wolf pinned him down. The animal's head reared back then let out a growl, saliva dripping down onto its victim's face. "Wyatt, no, please! She's going to be fine! She's just passed out."

The wolf opened its mouth, baring its teeth, then came down on Maxim's head with a snarl.

"Wyatt, don't!"

Wyatt's wolf was centimeters away from Maxim's neck when it stopped. It kept its massive paws on Maxim, but looked over its shoulder.

"Don't kill him." Arch Jones stood behind them, his imposing stare cool and collected. "Not yet," he added with a murderous glance at Maxim. "We need him alive so he can tell us what he used to subdue Lizzie."

"She's still out!" said the second man who held Lizzie's body in his arms. The wolf let out a growl, but Wyatt calmed it down as he recognized the man as Jacob Martin, Lizzie's younger brother.

Give me our body back, he pleaded to his wolf. *Please. We need to save her.* The wolf hesitated for a moment before releasing its hold. As he turned human again, he hauled Maxim to his feet and shook him by the collar. "What did you give to her?"

"J-just a sedative. S-something I read that works on your kind."

Wyatt ground his teeth together. "Only continuous intravenous anesthesia can knock us out completely. She should have burned off any sedative you gave her by now." He wrapped his hands around Maxim's neck and squeezed. "Tell me before I crush your windpipe and spine."

"B-belladonna! I bought it from a witch in Delaware," he cried. "Please ..."

"Motherfucker!" Jacob cursed.

Wyatt let out a ferocious roar, then tossed Maxim toward Arch before dashing over to Lizzie. "No ... please." Gently, Jacob handed her over, and he held her unmoving body to his chest.

Jacob pulled out his phone. "I'll call The Enclave medical wing."

"I should kill you right now, you stupid bastard," Arch said to Maxim in a menacing tone. "Belladonna isn't a sedative. It's poisonous to us! If she doesn't get the antidote in time, she's going to die."

Blood drained from Maxim's face. "I didn't know! I

swear, I only wanted to sedate her. I read on the Internet it can incapacitate your kind."

Arch let out a disgusted sound. "Do you believe everything you read online? I thought you were a tech genius?"

Please don't die, Wyatt begged as he cradled Lizzie in the crook of his arm and cupped her pale cheek. Her breathing was dangerously shallow. "Jacob?"

The other Lycan put his phone away. "Medical is on the way. Let's take her upstairs, back to your place," Jacob said in a somber tone.

He lifted Lizzie into his arms, carrying her back into his apartment building, ignoring the stares from the doorman and concierge. Jacob was babbling, trying to explain something to him, how Arch figured out Maxim was the one trying to breach into Creed's networks, but Wyatt was too focused on Lizzie's faint heartbeat to listen to him.

Jacob followed him as he rushed Lizzie into his bedroom, laying her down on the bed, then knelt beside her, taking her limp hand in his. "My Lizzie. My beautiful Lizzie." Movement under her eyelids made hope spring up in him. "You can fight this. Don't leave me. I'm never going to suppress my wolf again, Lizzie. You were right. I'm sorry."

But she didn't answer, lying perfectly still.

"Jacob!" he barked. "Is the antidote on the way?"

"Medical are on it, they're rushing it here," he said. "I'm trying to see if I can contact Daric or Cross." The warlock and his hybrid son both had the power to teleport across long distances. "Afterwards, I'm going to call Mom and Dad." His voice broke. "Stay with her, okay? Keep her comfortable." Fishing his phone out of his pocket, Jacob strode out of the bedroom.

Wyatt had never felt so powerless in his entire life as he did now, watching Lizzie cling to life. He wanted to swear, scream, and destroy things. His wolf, too, wanted to tear Maxim Silver's head off.

"Lizzie?" His head snapped up as her body began to convulse. "No!"

"Daric's here!" Jacob exclaimed as he burst through the door. Behind him, a tall, older man with long blond hair followed.

"Thank God! Do you have the antidote?"

"No time. I'll take her to the Medical wing." The warlock rushed to Lizzie's side, then took her hand. In an instant, they were gone.

"She'll be fine." Jacob gripped his shoulder reassuringly. "My sister's a tough one."

"I know. Thank you."

"Mom and Dad are on the way here, but I'll let them know to head over to The Enclave instead. Arch is taking Maxim Silver to the human authorities. Why don't you get dressed and then we can head over to The Enclave?"

In the rush of activity, Wyatt had forgotten that his clothes had ripped when he shifted into this wolf.

His wolf.

It was back!

He could feel it again, whole and free. One and complete.

The elation lasted only for a moment as he thought of Lizzie fighting for her life.

"That would be great. Thank you, Jacob."

~

The Enclave was a complex of buildings on the Upper East side where most of the New York clan lived. It functioned like a mini-city and was protected by magic so as to ward off their enemies, as well as curious humans. Thankfully, despite the revelation of their secret, the spells and protections around The Enclave remained intact, though they had been strengthened in the past few months. After all, because of their small numbers, Lycans did not mess around when it came to protecting their pups.

Wyatt followed Jacob from the parking garage, all the way up to the medical wing of The Enclave. Daric and Quinn and Selena Martin were already there in the waiting room, and much to his surprise, so were his parents.

Jade immediately embraced him as he walked in. "Selena called me. I'm so sorry, Wyatt."

The fear and anxiety eased in him as soon as his mother's arms and scent enveloped him. "M-Mom." His voice shook. "I don't want to lose her."

"Why the fuck did that bastard try to kidnap her?" Sebastian roared.

"Like I told Wyatt earlier," Jacob began. "Maxim was the one who breached the systems at Creed. He got in through a Trojan horse from a device that connected to one of his Wi-Fi systems, then hopped onto a home network linked with Creed."

The bottom of Wyatt's stomach dropped. "It was me. I connected my tablet to his Wi-Fi when I went to his house in Miami." Lizzie had been right to be suspicious.

"He didn't get too far, but he knew what he was looking for," Jacob continued. "He trawled through some Guardian

Initiative files in the trash that hadn't been emptied, which is how he must have found out about her powers."

"Arch saw him sneak a picture of Lizzie's laptop screen with his phone the last time Maxim came for a visit. We reviewed the footage several times to confirm, and so Arch decided to put a tail on him."

"We followed him the entire weekend," Jacob said. "He'd been waiting outside Wyatt's building the whole day. When Lizzie came out, we saw him go after her. He injected her with the belladonna and tried to drag her into his car. Thankfully, Wyatt was faster and stopped him."

"I think he wanted Lizzie to help him with his company." Quinn gritted his teeth. "I did a more thorough background check on Silver Securities Tech Worldwide. Turns out it's all a sham. His products don't have the capabilities he's been bragging about, and his investors were breathing down his neck. He probably thought Lizzie could get his tech to work."

"Bastard," Sebastian muttered. "Do we really have to turn him into the police?"

"Believe me, I want to kill him myself for what he's done to Lizzie," Quinn added. "But you know the rules. He's human, so he has to be dealt with by his own kind. Don't worry though, we have enough evidence to bury him, and we'll turn it over to the DA. Creed can file a civil suit, too, for espionage."

"Plus, there's the attempted kidnapping and murder charges," Jacob added. "I hope he gets put away from a long time."

Wyatt's chest ached. "Do we know anything about her condition?"

"She's with the doctors now," Selena said, her voice strained tight. "They're doing what they can."

Wyatt sank down into the nearest sofa, the initial rush of adrenaline now leaving his body. "This is all my fault."

"Maxim Silver was the one who gave her the belladonna," Jade reminded him as she sat down next to him. "He's to blame."

"But I drove her away." Fishing the ring from his pocket, he opened his palm to show it to his mother. "She gave it back ..."

Her eyes widened. "Wyatt, what happened?"

In all the worry and rush, Wyatt had almost forgotten about Fiona. "Mom ... Grandmama came to see me."

Jade's lips pressed together, and her entire body tensed.

Sebastian rushed to his mate's side, placing an arm around her. "What did that bitch want?"

Wyatt was taken aback by his father's words. Though there was no love lost between Fiona and his father, he'd never heard him say anything bad about her. "She wanted me to come back to England." And so, he explained everything that happened earlier that evening.

Jade's face crumpled. "Wyatt, I'm so sorry she did that ... and the things she said to you and Lizzie. It's unforgivable."

"Mom ... is it true? What she said about you and ... and your wolf?"

His parents looked at each other, and Wyatt knew that Fiona had been telling the truth. "Why—" He halted when the door to the treatment rooms opened. "Doctor!" He was on his feet before anyone else. "How is she?"

Dr. Blake, the clan's resident Lycan doctor, scratched at

his head. "I don't know how to explain it, but she's perfectly fine."

Tears of relief gathered in Wyatt's eyes. He tried to say something, but feared he would fall apart. A hand slipped into his and gave him a gentle squeeze. He didn't have to look down to know it was his mother's.

"Thank goodness you were able to give her the antidote in time," Jade said.

"That's just it." Dr. Blake's mouth pursed. "We didn't get a chance to administer the antidote. When Daric brought her here, she started convulsing and burning up with fever. It's like her body was neutralizing the poison by itself. I don't know how it could have happened."

Jade and Selena exchanged looks, before the latter spoke. "Doctor, is my daughter awake? Can we talk to her?"

"She's very tired, but seeing as she'll make a full recovery, I don't see why not. But not all at the same time, unless she feels up to it."

Daric cleared his throat. "If you all don't mind, I'll head out and tell everyone the good news about Lizzie's recovery."

"Thank you, Daric," Quinn said. "For getting her here."

The warlock nodded, then disappeared into thin air.

Even though Wyatt desperately wanted to see her, he hung back as Lizzie's parents followed Dr. Blake back into the treatment rooms.

"How are you feeling?" his mother asked.

"Relieved. And scared." He'd hurt Lizzie by not defending her against Fiona. He saw that now. "But she's alive, that's all that matters."

"Don't worry, darling," Jade soothed. "I'm sure everything will work out." She pulled him down to sit beside her.

Unsure what else to do, he put his head on her shoulder like he used to when he was a child. Her scent of vanilla and cherries comforted him and his wolf. *She's going to be okay,* he told his animal. But whether she would take him back was another matter.

"Wyatt?" Selena called when she appeared in the doorway a few minutes later.

"How is she?" Wyatt shot to his feet.

"She's fine." The corner of her mouth tugged up involuntarily. "Getting stronger by the second." Once again, she and Jade locked eyes knowingly. "She's asking for you. And you too, Jade, Sebastian."

"Us?" Jade asked. "But—"

Wyatt didn't bother to stay to hear his mother's questions as he brushed past Selena and into the treatment area. Jacob and Quinn were leaving the third door on the left, so he made a beeline toward them. When he entered the room, his gaze immediately drew to the figure in the bed.

"Lizzie." It was difficult to get her name past the lump in his throat. "H-how are you feeling?"

She was sitting up in the bed, propped against some pillows, her curly red locks spread around her shoulders. Her face was pale, but much better than when he last saw her.

"Wyatt," she croaked.

"Do you need anything? Water? Food? Blankets? I can call—"

"No." She shook her head. "I just need you."

He was at her side in a split second. "Lizzie." He could barely breathe. "Lizzie, I'm sorry. Please forgive me."

"Forgive you? Oh, Wyatt." She opened her arms. "Come here."

Indescribable joy shot through him as he collapsed into her arms. "Lizzie. My Lizzie." Nuzzling her neck, he breathed in her scent. "Please don't leave me again. I'll do anything for you. I promise. You'll never hear from Fiona. She's out of our lives. What she did and said was unforgivable."

"I'm sorry she hurt you so bad." She rubbed his back. "And—oh! Your wolf."

"Yes." He smiled at her. "It's back. I went crazy when I saw that bastard try to kidnap you."

She placed a hand over his chest. A deep rumble came from somewhere deep within him. "Oh, hello."

His wolf greeted her with an excited yip.

"I can't wait to see him again."

"And he can't wait to see you." *Thank you for saving our Lizzie.*

His wolf answered with a delighted bark.

"I'm just glad you're okay." He kissed her softly. "Do you know what happened? How were you able to metabolize the belladonna without it killing you?"

"Yeah, um, about that—"

"Lizzie? Wyatt?" Jade's head poked through the doorway. "Your mom said you wanted to see us?"

Lizzie straightened up and brushed her hair out of her face. "Yes, thank you for coming."

"We're just so glad to see that you're fine." Jade strode toward them, Sebastian right behind her. "I think I know why you want to speak with us. It's about my mother, isn't it?"

"Yes."

"We don't have to talk about her." Wyatt slipped an arm around Lizzie's shoulders. "We never have to see her or even think about her ever again." He would make sure of it. No one would ever hurt Lizzie again.

"Not talking about it is what got us here in the first place," Lizzie said wryly. "Mr. Creed, I think you owe Wyatt an apology."

"Excuse me?" Sebastian asked, his tone incredulous. "I wasn't the one who forced her child to hide who she was and broke her wolf."

"But you did push Wyatt away, even if you didn't mean to."

He huffed. "He wanted to go to school in England and build his life there. How could I stop him from pursuing his dreams? He always wanted to be the best. And then he did all those things I could only dream of—getting into that school, graduating with honors, finishing his MBA—it made me so damned proud."

Lizzie's eyes narrowed. "But did you ever tell him that? Did you ever tell him you were proud of him?"

"He knows it." Sebastian turned to Wyatt. "Right, son?"

Wyatt looked at Lizzie. How did she know?

"He does, but you never said it, did you? Not like you do with Bastian."

"I—" His father stopped short, his face slackening. "I never ... I mean ... son ..."

"Sebastian." Jade squeezed his arm. "She's right. You were always pushing Wyatt. You've been hard on him since the beginning."

"He's my son. My *firstborn* son." Sebastian gritted his teeth. "I couldn't ..." He swallowed hard. "I couldn't fuck up. Not like ..."

"Not like your dad did," his wife finished. There was no blame or anger in her tone. Just understanding.

Sebastian massaged his temple with his fingers. "Son, I pushed you to do well in everything you did—school, sports, after-school activities—because I didn't want you to be like me. Dirt poor, never went to college, no future. The only way I was leaving that trailer park was in cuffs or by joining the Marines." He circled around the bed to face him. "I wanted so much more for you. And you went on to do so many great things, things I could only dream of for myself. I'm so sorry I pushed you so hard. And I'm sorry I never said anything, but I am so fucking proud of you. Every Goddamned day."

"I know, Dad." He swallowed hard. "T-thank you for saying it."

Sebastian pulled him in for a fierce hug. "Love you, son,"

"Love you too, Dad."

Jade cleared her throat delicately. "Lizzie, dear, would you like us to leave? In case, uh, you wanted to tell Wyatt *something* in private?"

"Tell him—oh." Her face turned as red as her hair. "Um, no, you can stay. You should stay."

"Tell me what?" Alarm bells rang in his head. "Lizzie, are you still hurt? Did the belladonna have any lingering effects? Are you still sick?"

"What? No." She caught his hands in his. "I'm not sick, Wyatt. Turns out ... I'm pregnant."

Wyatt blinked. Then his knees buckled. Thankfully, he was able to brace himself on the bed before he fell over. "P-pregnant?"

"Yes. I'm your True Mate, Wyatt." Her mouth widened into a smile. "That's why the belladonna didn't kill me. Our baby was protecting me." No one knew why, but females carrying their True Mate's child became invulnerable throughout their pregnancy.

Glancing over at his mother, he asked. "You knew, didn't you?"

"Selena and I both suspected as much when she spit out that drink." Jade made a face. "I couldn't even stand the smell of alcohol whenever I was pregnant."

Lizzie was his True Mate.

And she was going to have his pup.

His wolf let out a joyful, ringing howl.

"Lizzie." He buried his nose in her hair as cupped her belly, indescribable joy filling him at the thought that their child was growing inside her this very moment. "My Lizzie ... I love you so much. Tell me what you want. Whatever it is, I'll give it to you." Releasing her, he looked deep into her beautiful arctic blue eyes.

"I already have everything I want, Wyatt. You as my True Mate and our baby. But what about you? Do you have everything you want?"

"Not quite." He reached into his pocket and took out the ring he'd kept in there for safekeeping. "Will you marry me, Lizzie?"

Tears shimmered in her eyes. "Yes, Wyatt."

He slipped the ring back on her finger. "It's always been you I wanted, Lizzie. I only wish I didn't wait so long. That I didn't try to resist the pull."

"I was oblivious, but it seems everyone saw it but us." She glanced shyly at his mother, who only grinned back.

"No more regrets." He kissed her knuckles. "We have the future to look forward to."

"Definitely."

Wyatt slipped his arms around her and pressed his mouth to hers in a sweet, slow kiss. His wolf spun around and chased its tail in delight, then yipped at Wyatt, so smug and pleased with itself.

Oh yeah, you told me so.

And for once in his life, he didn't begrudge his wolf's happiness.

Epilogue

A few days later ...

Despite being her True Mate, fiancé, and father of her future pups, Wyatt Creed remained a mystery ... and still definitely topped with a dash of, what-the-fuck, man.

Take this instance, for example.

Said man burst into her office unannounced, saying, "Don't move."

Glancing up from her screen, all she could say was, "Uh, okay?"

"Come in," he called out into the hallway, then stepped aside. Two men entered, carrying in what appeared to be a full-sized couch.

"What the hell?" Lizzie exclaimed.

"Over there." He directed the men to the window, where they placed the sofa. After having them adjust the positioning several times, he finally said, "Perfect. Thank you, gentlemen."

"Can I move now?" Lizzie asked once they were alone.

"You may."

"Thank you." She then strode over to him. "What's this about?"

"It's a couch."

"I can see that." Her hands planted on her hips. "But what's it doing here? In my office?"

He nodded out the window. "It's raining."

The dark clouds over Manhattan were indeed pouring down on the city. "And—Wyatt!" She let out a squeak of surprise when he pulled her down on the couch with him, landing on his lap. "What are you doing?"

He nuzzled at her neck. "I believe I've checked off every item on your list now."

"My—oh." *Cuddling on the couch on a rainy day.* "Wyatt ..." Turning her head, she pressed her mouth to his. Her wolf let out a satisfied sound, preening happily at the attention of their mate. His wolf, too, let out a rumble of joy that made his chest vibrate. Since that time Wyatt finally allowed his wolf to be free, she'd sensed not only the animal's joy, but also peace in both man and animal.

Of course, that didn't mean their lives were any less exciting.

The last few days had been a whirlwind for them, but in a good way. For one thing, Maxim Silver was currently sitting in jail, waiting to be arraigned. Although he had an expensive defense attorney, the kidnapping and attempted murder charges—not to mention the fact that he was a flight risk— were enough for the judge to deny his bail request. Creed and Lone Wolf were also preparing a civil lawsuit, as were his investors, so suffice to say that even if he managed to dodge the criminal charges, he was going to be buried under a lot of litigation for the next decade or so.

But on a happier note, Lizzie had completely moved into Wyatt's penthouse. Wyatt had hired movers to pack up all her personal belongings, plus he gave her one of his five bedrooms so she could have her own office/woman cave. They also announced their engagement and True Mate pairing to the rest of the clan, and everyone had sent their congratulations as well as asking when they planned to have their wedding.

They hadn't made any plans yet, but Lizzie wasn't worried about that. To be frank, she would rather have a courthouse wedding with just the family, but she was happy to compromise with Wyatt on the matter. He did, however, get her an early wedding present—a scholarship in her name, for a student of Code Girls Academy, which included college tuition and an internship at Creed Security.

Wyatt shifted her so she was on her back, then kissed her full on the mouth, before trailing down to her neck and nuzzling between her breasts.

"Mmmm ... we better stop," she sighed. "I'm pretty sure my Dad won't appreciate having to watch us make out on the cameras."

He let out a grunt, but didn't get up. Instead he crawled lower, so his face was right at her belly, then pressed a kiss there before he relaxed against her. Lizzie noticed he'd been doing that a lot lately, just laying there with his face on her stomach, hand possessively on her hip. "You know, he or she doesn't even have a heartbeat yet."

"I know." His grip on her tightened. "I just … it doesn't seem real to me, but I know—and my wolf knows—that our baby is in there."

Lizzie didn't miss the way his body tensed. "Wyatt? What's wrong?"

"I've been thinking. About … about my dad. And our baby." He glanced up at her, his hazel eyes filled with emotion. "I just … I don't wanna fuck this up—"

"You won't." She interrupted. "I promise, you won't." Hauling them both up, she sat on his lap and melded their mouths together. His hands slid up her waist, and up to her breasts. Squirming on his lap, she felt his hardness brush against her core. "Wyatt, we can't."

"Right." He huffed. "I guess I'll have to wait until later."

"Unless we play hooky." She waggled her eyebrows at him.

"Sounds like a great idea. We can get a room—"

"Hey, Lizzie, are you—oops!"

Wyatt let out an annoyed growl, and Lizzie slid off his lap. "Who—Charley!" She shot up to her feet and dashed across the room to embrace her cousin. "Is it—what are you— why didn't you—" Excitement poured through her at the presence of her cousin, whom she hadn't seen in months.

"Lizzie, I can't breathe," Charley choked. When Lizzie let go, she took in a deep breath. "I'm glad to see you too," she chuckled, then looked over her shoulder. "Sorry for interrupting."

"It's okay. Wyatt, you remember Charley, Uncle Connor's daughter?"

"Hello, Charley." He stood up and brushed his hands down his shirt. "It's been a while."

"Hey, Wyatt. Sorry to crash in on your *afternoon delight*, though I should have guessed from what Olivia told me," she said in a teasing tone.

"It's fine," Wyatt grumbled.

Lizzie flashed him a grateful smile, then turned back to her cousin. "But what are you doing here, Char? Is The Douche Hole touring in New York?"

"I quit," she stated with a shrug.

"Finally!" Lizzie exclaimed. "I swear, I thought you had some form of Stockholm syndrome or something from the way you kept staying on even after what he put you through. You must have hundreds of job offers, yet you still—"

"I know, I know." She let out a breath. "I'll be fine, though. I'm just taking a little break, and I wanted to go back home. But, that's not the only reason I'm here at Lone Wolf." Her toffee-brown eyes darkened. "I need to see Uncle Killian. I need to ask a favor."

"A favor?"

"I have a ... friend. She needs our help. Very, very confidential. And a very, very VIP." She chewed at her lip. "Someone's stalking her, and she needs protection. It's a delicate matter, and no one can know about it. So that's why I thought I'd come here in person to see Uncle Killian."

"I'm not sure ... with what happened recently, he and Arch are gun-shy about taking on private clients." Lizzie thought for a moment. "But you are family, and I'm sure we can figure something out. I'll even come and help you convince them."

"Really?"

"Of course."

"That would be awesome."

"I can help too," Wyatt added. "And if it's a VIP client, Killian and Arch might want my input."

"Aww, you guys are awesome." She winked at Wyatt. "And I just want to say, I'm glad you finally decided to admit your feelings for Lizzie."

"What?" Lizzie gasped. "You knew too?"

"Only from Cliff," Charley chuckled. "Apparently, everyone involved in GI had some kind of betting pool about when he was going to grow some balls—er, confess his love for you. Anyway, I'm gonna go see if Uncle Killian is free."

"We'll follow along," Wyatt said. "Give us a minute."

Charley gave them a thumbs-up, then disappeared through the doorway.

Lizzie groaned. "I really am oblivious."

He grinned. "I still love you."

"Love you too." Lizzie bit at her lower lip. "Hopefully this meeting won't take too long." Her curiosity was piqued, though. Who was Charley's VIP friend, and who was stalking her? "But I really do like the couch, thank you. I just wish we had more time to cuddle on it."

"That's all right." Slipping his arms around her waist, he pulled her to him. "We have the rest of our lives to cuddle."

The End

About the Author

Alicia Montgomery has always dreamed of becoming a romance novel writer. She started writing down her stories in now long-forgotten diaries and notebooks, never thinking that her dream would come true. After taking the well-worn path to a stable career, she is now plunging into the world of self-publishing.

facebook.com/aliciamontgomeryauthor

twitter.com/amontromance

bookbub.com/authors/alicia-montgomery